Contemporary Cheerharan:

WOMEN FIGHTING INDIGNITY AND INJUSTICE

Maitridevi Sisodia

Gaurav Julka

First Published in 2022

Becomeshakespeare.com

One Point Six Technologies Pvt Ltd
123, Building J2, Shram Seva Premises,
Wadala Truck Depot,
Wadala (East), Mumbai 400037, India
T: +91 8080226699

ISBN - 978-93-5458-362-9

To all women; for, they do not relent in face of unrelenting challenges.

And to my maternal Grandma Late Niranjanakumari, my paternal Grandma Manoharkunvar and my mother Krishnakumari, three strong women who raised me to be courageous and compassionate.

- Maitridevi Sisodia

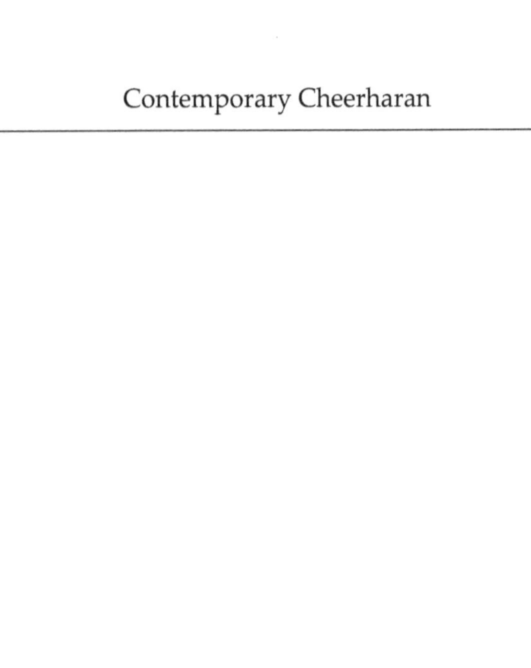

To every woman who has taken a stand and fought for her right. And to Rosa!

- Gaurav Julka

Preface

"The most awe-inspiring things in the world, started with the smallest of initiatives and at the smallest of places"

The idea of this anthology was born out of a simple conversation between us authors, as we were sharing our angst about the plight of women and the countless issues faced by them. We decided we wanted to express our infuriation with words, without sugar-coating anything and expressing reality as it really is - partly from experience and partly from observation.

This is a collection of works comprising of poetry, essays, short stories, diary entries, epigrams, open letters written by the co-authors.

A shloka in Sanskrit states that – "Yatra Nariyastu Pujyante, Ramante Tatra Devta", which means that the Lord resides in the land where women are worshipped. For all our lofty cultural ideals, the reality is pitiful. Gender bias and sexual harassment largely plague the lives of most women, holding them back. In this book, there are various emotional accounts based on some real stories, illustrating the hardships that are the unfortunate reality faced by thousands of women - be it dowry, domestic violence, acid attacks, forced prostitution or rape. In our book, you won't simply find short stories or straightforward open letters; we are here to represent our voice using art & literature in the hope that our country has eyes to gawk the reality.

We are here to enunciate.

We hope to throw light upon these issues, so we can all collectively agitate to change this repulsive culture of wronging women, which has set in like an indelible stain on our social fabric. We deserve better; we can do better; and, we must do better. Our society can only flourish when it is fair to all. This book is a clarion call to voice our concerns, fears and desires altogether for an India which is free from gender bias, where women do not have to settle for feeling unsafe as a way of life, where women have equal access to opportunities, where women aren't held back by fences, barriers and ceilings at every stage.

Introduction of the Authors

Maitridevi Sisodia is a civil servant based in Gujarat. She is part of Gujarat Administrative Services and is currently posted in Vadodara. An engineer by education, she has worked as a software engineer before joining civil service. She inherits her interest in literature from her grandfather Mr. Himmatsinh Sisodia, who has been her guide in all things literary. She is passionate about women empowerment and rural development. She believes that the pen bears power and has always yearned to write and create impact. She draws inspiration from Jane Austen; and Shakespeare is her favourite playwright.

Gaurav Julka is a senior manager at an MNC and currently based out of Singapore. He hails from Ruskin's Dehradun. A computer science engineer by education, Gaurav has developed his knack in writing through his blogging hobby. Gaurav finished writing the selected works of the anthology in 2014. He draws inspiration from Robert Louis Stevenson, William Ernest Henley; and Ruskin Bond is his favourite poet.

Acknowledgements

First and foremost, we're thankful to Become Shakespeare publication and the Wordit Art Fund for encouraging us amateur authors, and for helping us accomplish the publication of our first book. We're grateful to Shreyas Prathamshetti, our project manager and Reshma Kulkarni, our editor; they have been immensely helpful throughout this journey.

This passion project was envisaged a long time ago. For their faith and unwavering support since the early stages, we express gratitude to Akshata Naik, Ayushee Mishra, Dishi Solanki, Megha Saxena and Sharmin Vohra.

Special thanks to Mr. Digvijay Singh for helping us realise our vision for the Cover Design and for beautifully bringing it to fruition.

Contents

Cheerharan through the ages - Prose

-Maitridevi Sisodia

In the ancient Indian Epic "Mahabharata", eponymous to the war fought between Kauravas and Pandavas, Queen Draupadi's Cheerharan is the trigger for the war. In Hastinapur, prince clans of Kauravas and Pandavas play a game of dice. This treacherous game culminates into Pandavas losing their army, empire and all their wealth. The last bet is placed upon the honour of Pandavas' wife, Draupadi. Upon losing this bet, Draupadi is dragged out of her chamber by her hair and brought to the court to be disrobed. Devastated, Draupadi makes desperate pleas for help, questioning the right of her husband to put her at stake. She cries lividly, begs to save her modesty. Everyone is dumbfounded. This sombre episode from Mahabharata depicting Draupadi's wrath, evokes reactions of the same tone; numerous poems, essays and books have been written on the grave injustice done to Queen Draupadi.

Queen Draupadi's Cheerharan holds the mirror to a society, which was so degenerated that a Queen could be disrobed in presence of the best of scholars and warriors, who watched on silently without any fruitful protest. Many of these spectators were some of the finest men of the epic; their silence is one of the reasons that such a gross assault on Draupadi's dignity could be attempted. Drawing a parallel to our world, a lot of assaults on women's lives and dignity can be attributed, in part, to the silence of the spectators. Just as in the epic "Mahabharat", some characters justify the outrageous decision of King Yudhishthira to stake Draupadi, as he was just following the rules of the game and that a wife belongs to her husband. Thus, in our world as well, one can issue limitless justifications of the callous circumstances that women find themselves in. The lack of acknowledgement of the gamut of issues faced by women, and the astoundingly unfair patriarchal conditioning of accepting these issues as way of life, should make everyone indignant, like Draupadi.

It's an unfortunate truth but a gender toll is exacted at all stages of womanhood. Even before birth, a female foetus faces foeticide, so to say this gender toll is faced by women even before they come to exist in this world. Oh, the unfortunate weight of being a woman! For many who escape this perilous fate - lack of equal nutrition and education comes right up in their early years. The pressures of conforming to certain social practices standards, are also faced by young girls. Needless to say, most of these practices are regressive, rigged against women. Even the ones who relentlessly fight against skewed education and employment opportunities, face the injustice in terms of unequal pay. Most positions of power and prestige are held by men, even when there are more women than men in the world. Nobel Prize winner Wangari Maathai said, "The higher you go, the fewer women there are". This is but the gender toll, ever present. Women are also more vulnerable throughout their lives to sexual violence. More than a third of women globally have experienced physical or sexual violence. The drastic impact on their physical and mental health cannot be overstated. Gender toll manifests itself in many shapes and forms, but is recurrent in a woman's life. It is hard to imagine any woman completely escaping this toll, even in the most progressive parts of our world. What a ghastly reality!

When we talk about this gender toll or women issues, we talk about systemic problems that affect all of humankind, not just women. Women are the victims in most cases, but these acts mar the very fabric of the society. It is a travesty that our society finds a way to brutishly obliterate even a discussion on these matters, boxing them as feminist issues, with heavily negative connotations assigned to that word itself. By belittling the real issues, mocking and silencing those who raise their voices against them, our prejudiced system protects the perpetrators.

Quoting a couplet from a powerful poem by Pushyamitra Upadhyay –

"तुम ही कहो ये अश्रु तुम्हारे,

किसको क्या समझायेंगे?

सुनो द्रोपदी शस्त्र उठालो, अब गोविंद ना आयंगे|"

The poet asks Draupadi what her angry tears would mean to anyone? He urges her to pick up the weapons and defend herself as Lord Krishna (Govind) would not come to her rescue.

In all possibility, the act of Draupadi's Cheerharan could just be mythological but is emblematic of the atrocities and oppression that women continue to face throughout the documented human history. It is symbolic of the grave injustice done to all womanhood, albeit in different forms. It's a cataclysm, that even in 21st year of 21st century, women are expected to be "the second sex", subordinate to men. In this book, we voice our angst against all forms of this perpetual Cheerharan of women.

The platform with No number – Short Story

-Gaurav Julka

Rare are the times when something or someone inspires you beyond belief. Such awe-inspiring moments are unique and profound; they will always exist as a close, sacred memory in our powerful minds. I had the opportunity to experience such a rare inspiring yet scary moment during my first trip to Mumbai.

Mumbai, the maximum city; the city of echoing dreams. Mumbai can be this one city which can endow you with an experience beyond imagination, especially for the first-timers. It was the end of 2007, the extraordinary month of December; I was required to visit the national office of my student-run organization.

Being a computer engineer in India was an accustomed deal back then. I was in the first year of my college enjoying the profound freedom of being one. I was also voluntarily involved with one of the biggest student-run organizations in the world. Well. at least, that's what the senior members of the organization claimed it to be *(I still don't know whether it's true or not).* Nevertheless, I was asked to report to the Mumbai national office with some local project reports.

Ah! Project Reports…Sounds all jazzy for a 1st year student to work on, yeah!

By the evening of 17th December, I was almost done with submissions and detailed auditing of all my reports; Mumbai had really treated me well. I was not cheated by a cab driver, I was not pushed out from a local train yet, I had survived my first clubbing scene at Polly's, I had no ill-fate encounters with any goons; everything was simply paradisiacal & inspiring, just as I had always imagined it to be. Mumbai, not the city but the supreme sense of living, it became my dream too.

After a prodigious tour of Mumbai and experiencing the extraordinary Mumbaikar life, it was time to bid farewell to this maximum city and end another splendid chapter in life. Life in Baroda was artlessly boring compared to a Mumbaikar's life but nevertheless, it was quite pointless of me to even think on those lines. I was stuck in Baroda for at least another 4 years.

December is a berserk month when it comes to travel and it sounds even more insane when I talk about booking train tickets for an AC berth. I was in the middle of a similar situation, even though I was very finicky about traveling in buses and sleeper class trains; that time, these were the only valid options I had. I chose to travel via the classic Indian sleeper class train which started from Bandra Terminus and would take almost 6 hours to reach Baroda. It was around 7:00PM when I took a cab from my office in Vikhroli for Bandra terminus. I was expecting heavy traffic, as suggested by Mumbaikars but that wasn't the case. I was at Bandra Terminus at sharp 7:45PM which was surprisingly very early. My train was scheduled to depart at 10:40PM, which meant I had at least 3 hours to kill. That called for an urgency of innovation to do something with very limited resources *(The Art of Killing Time!)*.

I was told that the train I was travelling in, runs only once a week and generally departs from either platform 3 or the last platform which was still to be given a number. This platform was generally a host to the typical Indian Malgaadis (goods-carrier train) and a playground for cricket fans living at the station.

I was at this unique platform by 8:01 and started scanning around in search of something alluring. Well, I was expecting too much; it was almost deserted, leave alone interesting; plus, the platform had this eerie feeling and smelled of ammonia. I found a comfortable 'seating area' on a cement slab almost at the centre of the platform next to a tea stall. I had this weird feeling; I would be safe there.

My Blackberry was about to die on me; now I had a serious scarcity of resources for killing time. Accepting things had started becoming a part of my corporate-ish student life. I started scrutinizing and observing my external physical reality. I saw a bunch of slum kids with an age group of 10-16 playing some out-of-the-world card game which was impossible to understand from such a distance. I was really touched by the sound of them 'being so happy'. Most of them were wearing tatters in place of clothes, but still, they were masters of the profound skill of being happy.

My eyes quickly noticed something awkward. There was a secluded compartment of a freight train across the rail lines; exactly in front of the tea stall. The right side of the compartment had something scribbled on it. It said 'ABANDONED' in bright white colour. Suddenly, I saw a person, maybe in his mid-forties, dressed in a typical corporate outfit, was zipping up his pants in sheer excitement while coming out of the compartment. That rather amused me. he looked really educated and well off. *Why would someone do that? Ah!*

The next thing I saw was ingenuously ghastly. Two minutes after he left, a small teenage girl, perhaps underage, came out of the same abandoned compartment. She was kind of talking to herself as if she was under the influence of something really powerful. For the next few seconds, I could not believe what I had just seen and even if believed it, I was unable to comprehend the same. It was obvious after a while that she was responsible for the sheer excitement of that corporate bastard. As my thoughts started going blizzard, my eyes were still focused on her. She crossed the rail lines and joined the group of boys playing cards.

I had hardly gotten over the bizarre reality when a boy amongst the group grabbed my attention with his victorious shout of him winning the game, slashing his hand across the girl's breast, and acclaiming his award. I knew the girl was in pain; I could see it on her face. *The girl was his reward? Really? Could that be a reality?* He had his hands on her breast till the other boys forced him to fallback. Soon there was an argument regarding the girl's possession. The kid who had won the game was a junior and was not 'entitled' to such riches. The boys started asking her for a sexual intercourse with such degraded words that I had never heard before. The discussion concluded when the girl shouted that *"she had just had it and was in no mood to do so again"*. While she was shouting, we had a brief eye contact for a second and I could not dare to bestow her with a second look.

I seriously got nerves. *Where were the cops? What happened to our culture? Where was I? Was I in some kind of misconception about this world or was I still dreaming a bad dream?*

I wanted to do something about it. **'But what?'** With an unexpected adrenaline rush, I stood up and shouted… *"What the hell is going on here? Leave her along. Go from here!"* I doubt anyone understood that, but nevertheless they all scattered. The girl walked towards the tea stall and started drinking something; I guess it was tea. A boy was still after her. Very cheekily, he came close, spread his hands across her shoulder and requested something in her ears (which I imagine was nothing else but an intercourse). All I could auscultate was them talking about something 'twenty'. *Wait a minute…was that the price she was quoting?*

I saw the boy tossing over a five-rupee coin to the girl and promising her something for later *(perhaps the second instalment?)*. She turned around with an irascible smile and ordered him to pay-up by tonight. This was purely beyond conviction. The girl had a cost price; that too 'Rs. Twenty'. They both came to some sort of agreement; the girl was busy drinking her tea while the boy had 'acquired' the permission to move his hand over her neck and breasts until the tea stall owner shouted at them. The girl crossed the rail lines and disappeared towards the main station; the boy started strolling after her.

After witnessing one of the most atrocious and horrifying events of my life, with high levels of pumping adrenaline and 'gathered' courage I strolled towards the tea stall, seeking some insight as to *what the hell was really going on around here.* What the tea-stall guy articulated almost made me cry. He said, "…*this is her job…when she came from Surat…she was really good at it…now she is no fun…*" He advised me to stay away from this 'mess'. *Mess?*

I started walking towards the main platform dragging my heavy bag along. I was looking for a Police Chowki. I think more than police, I was looking for a hope. *"To earn hundred rupees a day, she needs to have an intercourse with at least five customers? Fuck!",* such thoughts had taken over my conscious and sub-conscious mind. The reply from policeman was as expected; he too advised me to stay away from this mess. He said he would send patrolling personnel on that platform, and suggested that I should not file a FIR as it could mean 'great troubles' for my career.

In some way I felt God was testing me that day. I learned that my train was an hour late and would depart at around 11:45PM. I tried to distract myself with every possible resource I could find. Even though I wanted to focus on something else, my eyes kept looking for that girl at every corner of the station. The thought of her having forced, unwanted and dirty intercourse kept my mind occupied *"In some corner of the station, Rs. 20, earning money for a night meal…. Ah!"*

It was 11:10 and my search was of no use, I returned back to my deserted platform; with an exception of the tea-stall owner and few dogs, I could not spot a single living soul. In a spur of moment, the same voice touched my ears. She was running towards the tea-stall, calling off and strolling after the stray dogs on the platform. We both had our second eye contact and again, I had no courage to give her a second look. I figured there was no way that I could look at her, leave alone the thought of having a chat… *"Having a chat? Where did that come from?"* I was a step away from re-defining my culture and strength, a step away from discovering something called *"Fortitude"*.

Something happened. I called her by a random name and invited her to sit next to me. She bluntly replied back by saying *"that is not my name"* (*I knew that for a fact*) and ignored my invitation. I just knew what would work; I flashed a 50-rupee currency note and asked her to join me again. She eagerly accepted my supplication. The very next second, she was sitting right next to me with her hands on my knees.

I held her hand and requested her to keep it way. I took her by surprise by saying that *I would be paying her Rs. 50, if she promises to not do 'stuff' with that boy tonight.* She quietly took the money at first and then returned it back. She said, she had never *begged in her life and that was the reason she chose to live such a life.* I started blabbering about the 'negatives' of such a life (very naïve of me). Of course, she knew much more than I could think of. I told her that she could keep the money as I was 'satisfied' sitting next to her. She took the money and said, *"Thanks"*. Another shocker for the night - her thank you was not in Hindi but English. I was interested to know the source of her knowledge.

A Mumbai winter chill ran through my spine as she told me her story. She had studied in an English medium school in Surat till class 6th. Her family was killed in the 2002 riots of Gujarat and she was forced to move with her family friends to Mumbai where she was left alone to live a life of misery. She had tried working as a maid but it never worked. She was living at this station since 2005.

After a minute of awkward silence, I gave her whatever cash I had with me (around Rs. 200) and asked her to return to her village/city. She said nothing, she wouldn't take the money. I had tears in my eyes, her eyes were wet too.

She quietly stood up, accepted the money and started walking away. I could only move my eyes; I felt a brain freeze.

I yelled, "What's your name?" in English *(expecting a reply)* but she kept walking away as if I never existed in the first place.

Few minutes later I was sitting in the train, confabulating…wondering if Rs. 250 would change a girl's life?

The train started progressing…

Towards the border of the platform, I saw someone standing with a brown cardboard. It was her; she was holding a worn-out cardboard piece with "Aarti" scrawled over it in bold capital letters.

"Aarti", I muttered.

It's almost 4AM, have been scribbling about this incident for over 4 hours. Let's see if I can find some tea at the subsequent station *"Hmm…. Surat"*

Woman you are... -Poetry

-Maitridevi Sisodia

Happiness we promise you,
nor today neither tomorrow,

Woman you are, only meant to bear all the sorrow.

In any decision of the family,
we will never you consult,

Woman you are silently abide all the insult.

Dare you carry a girl child;
we shall only be caused gloom,

Woman you are,
with only a son you will our family bloom.

Cook for all; have your meal the last,
that's all the esteem you get

Woman you are,
born for tough grind and gulp the regret.

Do not go out or exercise your merit,
hope not to earn for your sweat;

Woman you are,
the four walls of home is the entire world you get.

Mother, wife, aunt or sister;
Getting respect is for us males so you don't bother;

Woman you are,
suppressed or used or discarded, we don't bother.

Widowed, raped, divorced, abandoned;
it was all your blunder,

Woman you are,
meant to face it all and still surrender.

A Love that touches the sky – Short Story

- Maitridevi Sisodia

I

Purvi opens the curtain. Soft sunlight embraces her, and she smiles as she beholds the magnificent sight of Burj Khalifa. She does a big stretch, feeling as tall as the building she's looking at. Her firm has rented this swanky apartment in Dubai with a coveted view, for their brilliant new consultant. She sips her coffee and just soaks in the peace. Life has been going well, she thinks. Her phone rings, *"Beta, why haven't you called yet? Did you have breakfast? Don't be lazy and make just your coffee your breakfast"* goes her concerned mother on the other side. Ah mothers, they never stop worrying about their children, no matter how grown-up, now do they? Purvi tells her she'll get something to eat at the cafeteria, as she is getting late for work. Finishing the coffee and the conversation, she starts getting ready for work.

Things have been going really well for Purvi. She had always been a sincere, hard-working student and that was finally paying off. She was earning big bucks, helping her family, and also finding time to indulge herself. From school to graduation, alongside the MBA entrance preparation and from graduation to MBA, she never had the time to enjoy, to be herself. Now, she finally had the luxury of leisure. She had a good set of friends but none of them were in Dubai, something she missed here.

When she wasn't at work, she'd spend most of her time chatting with or talking to Ravi. Ravi lived in Chicago, but the time difference never got in the way of their connection. She realized what they had was more than just friendship, especially given that they came across each other through a social networking website and had never really met in person. She didn't want to ruin a good thing by bringing this up, not yet. *"Not yet"*, she mutters under her breath, answering Ravi's text on her way to work. Ravi had texted, *"Before I go to bed, I want you to check the event link on your Calendar"*. "Coffee and Conversations", the event read. Without checking further details, Purvi asks him to go to sleep and stop with these silly invites; they'd anyway have their "virtual coffee hangout" over the weekend. Ravi called her, *"Did you even check the invite? I'm asking you out for a coffee in Dubai, this Friday."* Purvi squeaked, *"What? Are you kidding me?"* She is overcome with joy and excitement. The week passes by in anticipation. Ravi and Purvi meet for the first time, after 8 months of having virtually connected. There was not an ounce of nervousness in either of them. Everything was going perfectly well. Ravi was as caring and responsible as Purvi thought he was. Purvi's vivacious energy seemed to have strongly captivated Ravi. They decide to go for a walk around Burj Park. After a lovely dinner. Ravi pokes her, "So madame, how is the evening going so far?" Purvi quips, "It's going swimmingly well, monsieur". Purvi admits it felt like they've always known each other. Ravi feels the same. They give each other an excited, re-assuring look, only lovers would know. 10 minutes into the walk, with the sight of Purvi's totem Burj Khalifa, Ravi goes down on one-knee and proposes her, *"Darling, let's have a love that touches the sky. Will you marry me?"*. Purvi did not see this coming. It had been a joke between them; she used to say she wanted a love grander than her totem. She jumps and says yes. She couldn't believe Ravi would come prepared with a filmy proposal. Purvi wanted to bottle up the feeling of having lived this perfect moment in love, so she could cherish it forever.

They inform their families, who're more than thrilled to begin planning the impending nuptials. Purvi starts preparing her move to Chicago. She has decided it made sense for her to move as Ravi was a US citizen, with his family living there as well. She could see a bright, happy future with him in Chicago. Ravi and Purvi plan for their parents to meet in Dubai itself, soon after the proposal. Ravi charmed Purvi's parents Pankaj and Rima with his sensible, caring demeanour. Ravi's parents were most happy about their son having fallen for Purvi, who they approved of. Everything seemed perfect about this union, with both sets of parents blessing them. The date was set and they were to be married in Ahmedabad in two months. It was a perfect match.

Time was flying with Purvi planning her move to Chicago and the wedding preparations. At times, Purvi couldn't believe her fate. Her friends were giving her a hard time about this swift, almost-filmy engagement that they missed. Ravi was equally excited about starting their lives together. It's Purvi's last week in Dubai, before she goes back to Ahmedabad for her wedding. She is cherishing every moment in the city that gave her peace of mind, stability and love. *"I'll miss our conversations, Burj"*, she says, looking at the sky-scraper, her totem. Ravi tells her, sometimes he's jealous of this sky-scraper for how much time Purvi spends admiring it every day. She gets a call from her mother; she answers *"Why are you up so late, Maa? Everything okay?".* "Ah yes, we're all busy preparing here, but thought I'd inform you about the change in venue and such", Rima tells her. She goes on to tell Purvi that they received a call from Ravi's mother Sheela, suggesting the new venue and better arrangements. It was much more expensive than they had planned, but as Ravi was their only son, Purvi's parents thought this was a reasonable request. Purvi finds this most unusual, but agrees with her parents' views. Rima tells her, *"Lavish weddings, beyond one's means are as good as rituals for most Indian families. You don't worry about this, we'll manage. And yes, do not to bring this up with Ravi; it might lead to unpleasantness."* This conversation left Purvi unnerved but she took her mother's advice and didn't tell anything to Ravi.

With the wedding day approaching, demands from Ravi's family started increasing, more jewellery, and expensive arrangements were sought. Nobody saw this coming. Pankaj, Purvi's father, has already taken a loan for wedding expenses. Now he was borrowing big sum of money from his friends to fulfil the piling demands from Sheela. Purvi got to know about all this when she got home. She is beyond disgusted with this, and despite their best attempts Pankaj and Rima cannot stop her from brining this up before Ravi.

"How could you let this happen, Ravi? This is dowry. I thought we were both clear that we didn't believe in these regressive, reprehensible practices", a teary-eyed Purvi tells him. *"Purvi, baby, calm down. Tell me what's going on? Of course, I am against dowry, I am not aware of it, please tell me"*, Ravi comforts her. Upon learning that her parents have taken loans, sold her mother's ornaments to meet his mother's demand, Ravi is enraged, but he convinces Purvi that with the wedding so close, it'd be best to not make this an issue. He promises that once she is in US, he'll help her re-pay all the debt that her parents had to incur for the wedding. Ravi had always been a problem-solver, she thought. Even her parents were convinced that this was the right way. They did not want to risk displeasing her in-laws and endangering her marital fortune. Buried in debt, they happily fulfilled Sheela's demands, for Purvi's happiness. Amidst this hassle, the marriage ceremony takes place. Ravi and Purvi become man and wife. The families celebrate their joyous union. As planned, Purvi gets to work in Mumbai for two months till her green card application gets approved. Ravi flies back to Chicago with his family. Two months fly by. Purvi starts moving as much money as she can spare to help her father repay the debt. Her green card application gets approved

without any trouble; she's fortunate like that, and now she's ready to really begin her life with Ravi.

II

Ravi picks her up at the airport. *"Hello wifey, finally I've you here", he exclaims* handing her a deep red carnation bouquet. *"I've missed you, hubs"*, Purvi replies hugging him. She is filled with excitement about her new life. She hasn't landed a job yet, but with her experience it shouldn't take long. Also, she felt this would give her the opportunity to bond with her parents-in-law. They welcome her warmly. They tell her about the dinner they've arranged, so she can meet with the neighbours and their local friends. Purvi had her worries about settling in but everything is so perfect. She feels truly blessed. Her parents are relived and happy, knowing that their precious Purvi is happy in her new home. But soon, things start shifting after a few days. Sheela starts getting rude with her about house work. Initially it was just a stern comment, once in a while but it kept getting progressively worse. Sheela also took her ornaments, under the pretext of keeping them secure. Purvi caught a bad feeling with all this. Ravi wasn't as attentive as before, whenever she tried to tell him about Sheela's behaviour, he'd dismiss it as her misunderstanding.

Purvi felt maybe it was just the process of adjusting in a new family. It's natural to have little discomfort whenever such changes come by. All the things she had heard growing up, made her feel that the onus was on women to adjust in their new lives. She took it upon herself to iron out the differences with Sheela. She started working harder at her job hunt, while taking care of all household chores. However, nothing seemed to work with Sheela; she kept finding faults with everything that Purvi did. She treated her like she was a non-human entity. Day after day, Purvi's spirit was chipped away. Ravi's father, Piyush at times, sympathized with her but he was complicit in the atrocities perpetrated by Sheela. One night at the dinner table, Sheela reprimanded Purvi about her cooking and started cursing her parents for not having taught her better. Purvi couldn't take it anymore *"You shouldn't be the one preaching anything about what one has been taught. Your morals were tainted the day you pestered my loving parents for dowry."* All the rage she had been suppressing for weeks, now flowed out along with her tears. Piyush played the mediator and helped calm the tempers. Perhaps, he didn't want neighbours to get involved more than anything. Things took a turn for worse after Sheela told Ravi about the incident. She started deepening the rift between Ravi and Purvi. Ravi and Purvi had an ugly argument that night. Purvi told him everything she left unsaid since the past few weeks. *"I don't even recognize you anymore. Ever since I've come here you've gotten more distant; your mother makes my life hell. I cannot tell my parents and burden them any further. What happened to your promises about helping me repay them? Are you just a beggar like your mother? Your mother was a teacher, your father is a doctor, they've been living in US for 40 years, but what morals do they've to show for their education? You all have made my life hell. My poor parents are worried everyday about paying off their debts, thanks to me. I hate you; I hate myself. For the love of God, please think about what you're doing to me! You promised me the world, but you've shattered my will to even live."*

She did not imagine what was to come, in her worst nightmares. Ravi locked her in their room, confiscated her passport and other documents, so his mother could keep them away. When Purvi started banging the door and making noise, Ravi got more furious and slapped her. The same guy who made tall claims about being a feminist, was reduced to a cruel, abusive man. It did not stop there; now it became a practice for Sheela and Ravi to together beat her up, if she resisted or tried to confront them. She was kept locked in her room, with barely scrapings for a meal. Purvi could not believe the misfortune that had befallen her. She couldn't reach out to her parents, who started suspecting something as she hardly called them. She was utterly lost and directionless. Every waking moment, she wondered how she got herself into this obnoxious place. She couldn't shake off the horrible feeling that it was her fault.

Weeks fly by. Purvi, who had been traumatized mentally and tortured physically, was nothing like herself anymore. Her body was reduced to a bony silhouette, the bruises on her face would tell the truth about her condition if anyone laid one glance at her. But here she was locked away. Sheela managed to get her to ask her parents to gift a car to Ravi for his birthday; she complied. She had no will left to fight anything, anymore. Purvi would sometimes ask Ravi, if it was her fault that she loved him and believed him without any second thought. Ravi hardly paid attention to her tearful pleas. She was completely crushed, abandoned and alone, in this battle.

One evening, they had unexpected guests. Purvi was locked away in her room, but she could hear the commotion. Soon enough, Sheela came to her room, commanded her to fix herself and come out to meet their old family friends, who were visiting along with their newly married son and daughter-in-law. She was also threatened to not utter a word, beyond pleasantries. Purvi knew the cost of not following

Sheela's instructions all too well; the scars on her hands and face spoke volumes for it. She did the best she could. She wore a full sleeve dress, to hide her scars and put up some makeup. She thought to herself, just a few months back, she'd be putting on makeup to go on a dinner or clubbing with her friends and here she was, putting on makeup to hide the bruises on her face. She was disgusted with her reality, with her life, with herself.

Purvi goes to greet the guests, as Sheela had asked her. But she couldn't make a quick exit, as Sonia, their newly-wed guest, picks up a conversation with her about Dubai. Her husband and she had just visited there and they were told she lived their earlier. *"Ah, Dubai Purvi, she was a whole different person"*, she thinks to herself. She makes an excuse to go to kitchen to arrange refreshments, as Sheela gestured. Sheela was getting unnerved because the more Purvi stayed around people, the riskier it could be for them. Sonia follows her to the kitchen, despite Sheela's best efforts to prevent her guest. Purvi hasn't had a proper conversation in months and Sonia's warm presence works like a balm on her battered spirit. Sonia shows her pictures from her Dubai trip on her phone, *"Oh, that old friend, Burj"*, Purvi thinks. At that moment, she feels a shift in herself. It triggers a solid sense of alienation with who she had become, this broken shell of a person. She did not want to be that anymore. Talking to Sonia reminds her of her own chirpy self, which has been cruelly snatched from her. In that moment, she decides to do something about it; she owed it to herself and her parents. After getting a bit comfortable, Sonia asks her if she had been unwell. Anyone who took a good look at Purvi, would've had that question. Purvi starts crying, but before she can say anything, Sheela comes to the kitchen and sends her back to her room, under the pretext of her being unwell. Purvi hastily hands a tissue to Sonia, before retiring to her room, hoping against hope that Sonia does something about it.

The guests leave in sometime. Purvi has been waiting for this. She asks Sheela and Ravi to hand back her passport and documents and tells them that she wished to go back to India. This is met with arguments and abuse. But today, Purvi was not going to keep quiet; she started running towards the door. She screamed at the top of her voice, she demanded freedom. Soon enough, she was locked away again. In a few minutes, the doorbell rang; it was the emergency services. Sonia had alerted the emergency services, soon after they left. Ravi and Sheela tried their best to say Purvi was asleep, but she started banging from inside her room as soon as she heard the doorbell. She wasn't going to let this opportunity go; she had endured enough. The officers interrogated all of them. Purvi recounted the horrors that she had been living through, and the officers could put two and two together with one look. Ravi was arrested and Purvi was asked to stay with the neighbours she trusted. Purvi thought she'd feel a sense of freedom, but instead she only felt this heavy sadness; she couldn't stop crying. What had life come to? She had to get the person she loved and wanted to spend her life with arrested. Her neighbours were kind; they took care of her and asked her if she wanted to speak to her parents. She denied. She hadn't cleared her head yet and she didn't want them to worry. Piyush and Sheela requested to speak to her; she allowed it. For a few minutes, all of them were just crying, everyone was distraught. Sheela started pleading with her and apologizing to her. She promised her that they can all put the past behind and start afresh, if she helped them release Ravi. Purvi saw a ray of hope. She was tired of living this life and she still loved Ravi, even after months of being locked away. Love is a strange beast, after all. Sheela pleads her that if she gave a statement that she was mentally unwell and she had hurt herself, they could get Ravi back without any trouble and start a new life. Sheela even said, she'd move out along with Piyush to their Texas home, so Ravi and Purvi could live by themselves. The months of confinement and torture had taken its toll on Purvi. She realized that giving such a statement was a big prize but the promise of marital bliss with her lover outweighed her brief moment of concern. She agreed to this proposal. She gave a statement that she hurt herself but accused her husband instead. The very next day, Ravi was released. He apologized to Purvi and hugged her, promising her to mend his ways.

Sheela keeps her promise too. They return the passport and other documents to Purvi. All of them are apologetic to Purvi. She feels as though she was on the precipice of marital bliss, things were getting better. It had been two weeks since Ravi's release. Sheela and Piyush planned to shift to Texas by the end of month. The family went to dinners and drives. Purvi started believing in her love, again. She chose not to tell her parents about the arrest, she wanted a clean slate. Tabula Rasa. Ravi started helping her with her job hunt. Soon, she had interviews lined up for next month. Ravi suggests that they should visit her cousin in New York for the long weekend. She could fly in early and he'd join on Saturday. Purvi is thrilled; this is what they used to talk about, travelling together, taking trips on long weekends. Love does conquer all, she thought to herself. She couldn't be more excited. She was finally getting back to herself. Ravi plans the trip along with her; she flies to her cousin, two days early as decided. Purvi enjoys her time with her cousin. The few months that she spent in utter horror, start seeming like a distant memory. That's the curious thing about our brains; the weight of misery dissipates rather quickly if one gets one's hopes back. Purvi was full of hope, now. She couldn't wait for Ravi to land, so they could get on with their trip. Ravi had been busy at work, wrapping meetings so they could have the weekend to themselves. He texted her that he was stuck at work, as he couldn't answer her calls. It was Friday night, Purvi was impatient now.

"Hey hubby, I've been missing you. What time is your flight landing? I'll come get you at the airport", she says to Ravi, who has finally picked up her call. Ravi dourly informs her that he wasn't coming. She didn't understand at first, she thought he meant he had work. She offered to fly back so they could spend the weekend in Chicago, instead. To her great infelicity, Ravi tells her that he had filed for divorce, on the grounds of her statement that she was mentally unstable and that she would be getting the papers soon. Purvi was aghast at his cruelty. She howled; he disconnected the call before she could say anything. It had all been a ruse! She felt like the most foolish person on the face of the earth. More than the grief of being deceived by her love, she grieved the loss

of her sense of self and her dignity. If it weren't for her cousins, she might not have survived. She slowly gathered the broken pieces of herself. Her parents gave her moral support and with therapy, she got better with time. She took back her job in Dubai, lives in a different apartment with her favourite view still, but she doesn't feel as tall as Burj Khalifa, during her morning stretches anymore. But her totem, as she calls it, is at her rescue again. *"A Love that touches the sky, just like Burj, but with myself this time"*, Purvi says. One day at a time.

Epigrams for an Indian Wife – Epigram/Quatrain

-Gaurav Julka

Dare you take that nibble of bread down your throat,

You're not being loyal; not a devote.

If you make a mistake of an early eat,

Won't have the privilege of his holy feet.

You're his to command; his to lead,

Act like one, you are from a woman breed.

Sex is a man's right; he needs that gain,

So, who cares if it's rough; and you're in pain?

Sacrifice is common; keeps you out of danger,

Even if it means that you are to sleep with a stranger.

He is selling you out; he is not insane,

He is doing it for you; for "us"; for a mutual gain.

Can you dress like that porn star? May be make
some noise,

That should be good; keeps you away from toys.

Lay like a doll; do you have a choice?

It's your responsibility; let the man rejoice.

It's because I am a man, I can dare to express,

You lady; don't have right…don't even try to assess.

She - Poetry

- Gaurav Julka

She never says it

But we know she wants to.

She never does it.

But we know she could.

She never asks for it.

But we know she deserves it.

Care. We never ask for.

But She always does.

One Last Time…One Last Night – Poetry

- Gaurav Julka

She stood infirm with every
inch of her body paralyzed,

For that matter, A Choice;
and she should have been in paradise.

Only if she could like...just go back in time,

And behold that humble request that he once made

One Malapropos decision;
that one unfortunate trade.

It did not have to be so bad;
it was just a victimless crime.

Galvanizing; Elementary.
Nothing else! It was just about a night.

That's what they said, "Take the Money"
and it's gonna be alright.

The value of respect vs. the value of a dime,

'Unaware' she was, it was going to be vicious ride

No way ceasing; like the full moon high tide.

More she wished, she could be sublime,

More the humiliation and dander took over her life,

She was the butter and her life a butter knife.

Not a ray of hope or a utopist sign,

Wish he was here;
the man of humility standing in white

Disposition in Life.
And now this life at the Red light.

Only if she had an eraser, she would rewrite;

"Hey you, Listen. Once last time, One Last Night?"

Sell me again...
-Lyrics/Poetry

- Gaurav Julka

Nights of tears, days of sorrow

Those forevermore messages that you send;

Could you hold my hand, make it end?

Endless wheel of life, passing time

Anhydrous my eye,

Search for thy rhyme

Is this the love that you meant?

Could you hold my hand, make it end?

Save me from satin, for what are you waiting?

Looking for a hope;

For what?

Life

That's no longer sane, make it end.

Hands to hold made the sold.

Price of my life;

Life

That's no longer sane, make it end.

If you were right, here by me;

If you try steer my thee,

Sell me again. Sell me again.

Women's Valour – Poetry

-Maitridevi Sisodia

Standing intrepid against

the mutiny of life every moment,

Hey Mister,

don't you dare your lady torment;

Violated and impugned, nay,

I have immense courage,

Treat me like a toy;

you shall be hosted by my rage,

And all you morons

ogling every girl that passes by,

Stop making those noises, or

noose on your necks we'll tie;

I feel blessed about my womanhood,

Pity, you'll never understand the way you should.

Nothing bitter like a woman's reprisal they say,

But there are million men like you, you all shall pay;

Dare you hit me and I'll break your face,

Try and trap me, be sure to be caged,

For I know I am a woman and you are a man,

But there is nothing that I cannot do and you can!

Caged Birds – Free Sonnet

-Maitridevi Sisodia

A lovely bird chirping in the woods
enjoying frolic of the sunlight,

Its splendour met the bird-catcher's eye,
and then you know its plight;

Bird-catcher brought the bird back to his abode,
grinning about his win,

He thought to himself,
it is a mighty addition and he will use to his whim.

The grand new bird in the brand-new world,
perplexed and anxious,

Said one of the old birds from the cage,
"You'll get used to it, don't be cautious",

There were all kinds of birds with the catcher,
red and black and yellow,

From different jungles and different places,
traded for tricks real shallow,

As the daylight shed and the darkness took by,
begun the unholy trade thereby,

The birds were all deprived of the sky and left in the
cages for the catchers to try,

Insuperable and non-evadable, the bird missed its
life in the skies and woods,

Some came some said, you can run away and start
afresh with your broods;

It's too late, felt the bird alike the thousand other
birds, it's too late to live;

This cage made me leave my life and from here
itself, the world I'll leave!

A Mumbaikar's Diary – Chick Lit

- Gaurav Julka

9th October, 2010. Saturday.

(Jobs: 1, Degree: 0, Cigarettes: 4 (before 9pm), 7 (after 9PM), Girlfriends: 1, Visit to Police Station: 1, Crimes committed: 0)

......

.....

...

5:30 PM: Damn!

5:31 PM: Late again. She will not forgive me this time!

5:32 PM: Fuck You! Pink shirt guy.

5:34 PM: People seriously need to learn how to behave in India. There is no sense of discipline, no sense of responsibility.

5:40 PM: Traveling in a Mumbai local during a peak hour is like striving for existence on this planet. It's almost impossible to find 'walking space' on Dadar station.

5:45 PM: Why do I have to do this? Vikhroli to Andheri every third day, just for 40mins. Ah! They say love makes you crazy of sorts…I shouldn't have written that…

6:10 PM: Two stops away from Andheri. It's almost impossible to write while you are traveling in the Mumbai local. Well, having a Smartphone helps. #Blackberry

6:18 PM: Andheri! Is this the feeling of being content? There she is. Would travel hundred times; like this, just to see her face and feel how I feel right now. (I need to stop talking to myself)

6:19 PM: Just realized. Watching too much Dexter & Lost could be one of the reasons why I have started talking to myself. [Point to be noted]

6:40 PM: Violet flowers; Cheese Cake.

6:55 PM: Carter Road, here I come. The last time I visited Carter Road, I was sloshed. I think, I had more alcohol in my body than blood. Janty Janty Ooo Ooo.

(Reminder: I cannot let a boy ever read this diary; judging will happen)

7:15 PM: Okay! This Rick guy was quick. 20 Minutes from Andheri to Carter. Dude! Let me check for NOS.

7:06 PM: It's always awe-inspiring to have conversations with her; mesmerizing type feeling. I wish I had more content on the topics she always wants us to converse on. I wish I read more.

7:25 PM: #Nowplaying Mai Ruka tha – The Local Train

7:31 PM: I am sure she is thinking that I am texting Rati J again and again; she has no clue about this crazy habit of mine

7:32 PM: #Nowplaying Good Life- One Republic

7:33 PM: *"Always and Forever"*, I haven't said that to her yet.

8:01PM: She must go to a party at 8:30? When was she planning to tell me…at 8:29?

8:25 PM: In a rick again; dropping her to a friend's house in Parle. Why am I not invited? Not that I want to go to his house, just wanna stay with her for a while…

8:35 PM: Dropped her to her friend's house. Will pick her up at 10:30ish, till then let's sort out the dinner scene...

8:38 PM: I should Tweet more often; express myself! This way I can learn more by practicing, writing. I really need to work on my English grammar. It's fucked up. Hopefully it will be sorted soon, who knows...someday I might just write my own book. For now, let's hit Juhu Mocha for dinner.

8:51 PM: Juhu Beach; An inspiring amalgamation of life with lights, food, people, sea and the sand. I think I should go for a Mumbai Special Pav Bhaji today.

 Food; India is all about food, it's about foodies, recipes, varieties and taste. The profound thing about the Indian food is its diversity. If you have not discovered what I am talking about...well...you're not really an Indian. (Reminder: I should soon find a place in Mumbai where I can get Daal, Baati and choorma)

8:58 PM: *"Boss, Ek plate Pav Bhaji... extra butter and cheese..."*

9:24 PM: Was this the best Pav Bhaji I ever had? I guess so (If I exclude the Pav Bhaji outside The Maharaja Sayajirao University aka MSU at Baroda – that one is simply exemplary)

9:35 PM: I still have an hour before I can pick her up from Parle. Aeee, what do we do?

9:41 PM: Decided to spend another hour at Juhu beach. Walk along the sea, talk to the winds, breathe some air (well, not that pure) and appreciate life.

9:52 PM: What the fuck was that? I just saw a couple doing more than just making out on the beach. Disgusting dude! Why would you do that on the beach? Oho!

You can't help it, can you? Couples here don't have the freedom to go to their respective homes and spend quality time with their partners. This is bound to happen. When you restrict someone's freedom they find 'unauthorized' ways to do what they want to do. Always will. Why do parents even restrict their children from dating? In today's age, almost every college going student dates…officially or unofficially. I have never understood the concept of protecting the culture when the culture is of no value and makes no sense.

9:56 PM: Kept walking along the beach. Found more couples 'destroying the values & culture of our country'. Wait! How come so many of them? Aren't they shy of each other? Why is that man walking away from that woman

9:59 PM: Fuck my life. She is masturbating him. Are you fucking kidding me? Every couple was doing the same. Fuck. What the fuck is happening? (I better keep walking and get the hell out of here)

10:01 PM: Why is that man standing behind the couple? Is he waiting for something…? Holy Fuck! They are no fucking couples! All the women here are Prostitutes.

Now I get it…It's a fucking 3D Holographic Brothel.

10:04 PM: There are at least 12-15 prostitutes around me. I am walking towards Versova and I better start running.

10:05 PM: Did she just…Disgusting dude! This one clad in a green saree just masturbated a jogger style guy…who walked away in supreme glory (no sense of guilt of any kind) …she just called in the next guy after washing her hands in the sea…like right next to her. I AM NEVER TOUCHING JUHU BEACH SEA WATER AGAIN.

10:10 PM: Spotted a Cigarette guy; a Milds would sort me out.

10:11 PM: Bought 'Choti Goldflake' for 6 Rs each. Fucking looters! Though I did get the information I wanted from him. I asked him what was all this?

What was going on around here? He said, "Dhandha re" … then I asked him, "Police doesn't do anything about it?" … His reply took me by surprise, "Saahabji, first time, right? It's okay. They get their cut"

10:16 PM: Well. If Police doesn't fucking do anything about it? I have no right to be Superman here. WALK AWAY.

10:18 PM: Started walking away from the 'dark side' of the beach towards the Mocha entrance. I thought I had left it all behind.

Insanity, <Something>, <Something> all have a limit. But this was beyond that. I just saw a woman dressed in a red saree with shiny glitter, slapping a girl (would be 13-14 tops) and forcing her to masturbate a random guy. I don't believe this. This is worse than standard prostitution. This is disgusting.

Wish I could help that girl…Wish I could do something about it…

10:21 PM: I wonder how much do they charge for 'one time'?

10:22 PM: Woah! Did I just see a guy wearing 'Nike shoes and Reebok shorts' doing that? Or I should write 'getting that done'. Hilarious yet sad that educated men of our society are part of the same. I wonder what his family thinks about him and what he really is.

What happened to the 'culture'? ...Fuck it.

10:24 PM: But it's worth to ask the price…

10:28 PM: Fuck! I just asked a thin woman (I think a girl) in pink salwar suit (with shiny glitter), " Kitna?" (That was all that I could dare to say)

Her reply synched with the jolt of the breeze came to me as a shock of my life. "100 ka aur 50 ka", she said. This was the cheapest prostitution rate I have ever heard of.

50 Rs ...that 13-yr old girl will earn 50 Rs after all that. Fuck!

I walked away, ignoring the pink girl's invitation (she was eager to bargain as well) I wish I could do something about it. I wish I could do something about that 13-year-old girl. I wish I could…

10:33 PM: Called Tashu, told her I will be late to pick her up. She was anyways having a time of her life.

These winds…

10:38 PM: That girl is almost the same age as of my sister. Fuck my life.

10:45 PM: Walked into the Juhu Police station, there was a gang of chillers and millers. Walked straight up to the guy with maximum stars…

"Sir, there is Dhanda happening towards that side of the beach"

His reply (not shocking yet), "Kaunsa dhandha?". I replied with obvious hesitation, "Prostitution". He genuinely replied (I hope that he did), "We will manage, thank you for the information".

So, I asked him…what was he going to do about it…? He said he was going to take a Jeep down there right now and see what's happening. I felt better. Some hope.

10:51 PM: I called up some of my team mates in Vikhroli letting them know where I am and in what 'mess' I could be. (Just in case)

10:52 PM: I requested the police guy to take me along with him in the jeep. He obviously denied the request and asked me to stay out of it. He never asked me to file an FIR or something…

11:00 PM: Fuck! I couldn't have found a blonder police guy. This guy brainlessly turns on the jeep light and siren and drives towards Versova. Dear Police Man, you won't find shit there.

Got a call from one of my team mates. He strongly suggested me to stay out of it...as all this 'shit' involved mafia gangs. I was happy that someone was concerned about me...but what about that girl? Who was going to be concerned about her?

11:15 PM: I was sure the police jeep would find nothing. With those lights and siren, even the dog knows that he is not supposed to poop there.

Well, I think this was the best I could do. Really...? The irony is that I am the Vice President Social Sector of the Indian <branch> of one of the world's largest student run organizations. I am responsible for all projects under social causes and this was the best that I could do?

11:20 PM: This is my 5th Choti Goldflake since dinner. I am not thinking about that girl anymore. I am thinking about **myself. Me. Youth. Young India**.

11:45 PM: At Parle, to pick her up. Will drop her home right away, I think I just need some sleep to get over it. This experience is just another experience in the list of 'Indian Experiences' one could have in India. I can do nothing about it. Not now at least.

10th October, 2010 Sunday

(Jobs: 1, Degree: 0, Cigarettes: 2, Girlfriends: 1, Peace of mind: none)

12:24 AM: Told her all about it. She didn't quite react. I think it's common for a Mumbaikar to hear about all this. It's a part of their Mumbaikar lives. Dropped her home, heading for Vikhroli.

01:10 AM: The much-needed bunk bed. The much-needed sleep. And maybe someday, a much-needed change in life style!

.....

Because she still has the courache –Nonsense/Poetry

-GauravJulka

Fighta like a **hero,** what did I just say

Romance thy chance; a defined cultural-ish match

She will try, even if the flowers don't sway

Because she still has the courache

Rocka like a solid, up goes her nose

Sundance thy glance; a defined sad-ish fame

Saturated with anger; the fire hose

Poking around; looking for a last name

Burna like a fire, they engulfed the rain

Flames thy power; such a man-nish chase

Nor the curve-ish projection or the tangent plane

Walking around without a sack; still in a sack race

Shielda like a titanium, she stood up-sage

Fierce thy stance; a defined try-ish attempt

To save herself; from keeping her back-stage

And to make herself exempt

Uselessa like a speck of sand, she lost the battle

Give up thy chance; such a woman-ish space

Made of shame; even scared to rattle

Burn thy tail; as if it might turn into a wing case

Fighta like a **hero**, what did I just say

Romance thy chance; a defined cultural-ish match

She will try, even if the flowers don't sway

Because she still has the courache

"It's a girl" – Epigram/Poetry

-Maitridevi Sisodia

The doctor said, "It's a girl",
and there took the world an ugly swirl;

Oh, she is an unholy burden,
how will you afford her marriage all sudden;

Don't educate her, what's the need?
Housework is job for woman's breed;

Oh, why give her freedom so much;
as if she will win the world as such,

She gets a job, don't let her go,
which man shall abuse her you never know,

Self-dependence for a woman?
Oh, what is that, in vain but she will never get,

Don't feed her much on self-respect,
her husband owns her that's her prospect,

Hustle for the family without hassle,
you are not a princess this isn't your castle;

Don't raise your voice we don't pay heed,
give us a son that shall be a holy deed,

Your family will pay for our demands,
we traded our son to you so no remand,

Unfortunate that woman carried a girl foetus,
forced to abort or be abandoned;

The woman chose the harder path;
she felt it's better to be left than cause death,

So again, she was a new life aboard,
free from slavery and all that throb;

And the doctor said, "It's a girl",
and her world took an affable swirl.

Saga of the pristine woman – Epigram/Poetry

-Maitridevi Sisodia

Pristine woman is so sure,

serving her man is all it takes;

To climb up the heaven,

her family is her only stake,

Her man but never

does her pure heart count

To him, it's her duty

and that is all that accounts;

Sad is such a relation,

a deadlock in its way

No one counts for the pain,

which the woman's heart sways

And then the world mocks

her household chores,

Lest no one knows, t

o her sea those are the only shores;

She weeps in nothingness,

hoping her children will be her nest,

For all that she does,

they seldom grow up with gratefulness,

A loyal wife, a devoted mother;

whole life enduring the cruel world's smother

Reap to her harvest is being

a disdained wife and a scorned mother.

Toil and work and weep and bleed,

she doesn't show what lies below

Unfolding innumerable layers of care,

all she does is her pride swallow.

Scars of Spite – Short Story

- Maitridevi Sisodia

"80 bucks is too much, Bhaiya", Maya tells the cab-driver, as she hands over the change to him. On any other day, she would have haggled over this bloated cab fare and paid the fair price, but she is in a hurry to get to her apartment. Dressed in a striking black dress, she is getting back from a successful rehearsal for the grand fundraiser at her college but her countenance betrays no pleasant emotion. One look at her, even as she moves briskly, would tell one that she is disturbed and stressed. *"Ah perfect, the lift is out of order for the Nth time this month, Good God!"* she mutters under her breath as she starts pacing up the flight of stairs, a little too fast. Her phone starts ringing. She barely saves herself from slipping but reaches into her bag to get the phone. "Unknown number" flashes on her phone; best to ignore this. Her heart starts pounding faster, she wonders if it's the stairs or the stress; she knows better.

She wheezes up the stairs to her 8th floor rented apartment that she shares with 3 other women. She locks the door behind her and feels a sense of slight relief descending upon her as she catches her breath. Vinny, her flat-mate, calls from the kitchen, *"Is it you, Maya?"* Maya goes into the kitchen, gives half a smile to Vinny, grabs a water bottle and before she can turn around, her phone rings again. That sense of relief vanishes as quickly as it descended. "Unknown number". She now knows it has to be him. Maya purses her lips, as she contemplates whether to pick up and confirm her worst fear. She rejects the call and blocks the number. She has had enough. Vinny pieces things together looking at Maya consumed by a sense of fear, *"Is it him? Did something happen, M? Are you alright?"* Maya who feels fear, disgust and grief weighing her down, all at once, bursts in tears *"He tried to follow me home, Vin. Third time this month. I don't know what to do anymore. He just won't budge."* Vinny comforts her, *"Babe, you need to register a complaint with your university or police, or at least tell your family about how Sapan has been bothering you. He seems incorrigible. Look at what he's doing to you. You don't deserve this. You were a good friend to him but look at this ungrateful loser."* Maya is lost, she is drowning in a fog of dread, she can listen to Vinny's words but her faculties cannot grapple with them. Vinny coaxes Maya into having dinner with her. She merely nibbles a bite or two, talks about the fundraiser to take attention away from her stalker, before feigning sleepiness.

Maya gasps loudly, as she closes her bedroom door. It's a good thing she has the bedroom to herself for now, she thinks. Tanya, who shares the room is on a vacation. Perhaps she should work on polishing her performance for the fundraiser. She was not just the lead vocalist for her college band but also headed the Organizing Committee, putting the event together. There were several final day details she should be fretting over right now, yet she was not able to focus. She tries to shake off her preoccupation and makes a few team-calls to iron out necessary details. It helped that she got heaps of compliments on her rehearsal performance. Kind words and pat-on-the-back friends always serve as the quintessential pick-me-ups, don't they? The prospect of a successful event almost makes her forget the stress. Maybe she should stop thinking about it and fight this battle another day. Clearly, she had a lot on her plate for the next day. She listens to a few upbeat tracks and makes up her mind to not give Sapan another thought. She changes into her jammies and prepares for one last solo practice before nodding off. Her phone rings again. "Unknown number" flashing. All her efforts from the last hour to put this behind go right down the drain. She could feel the anxiety buzzing to her bones, as the phone continues ringing.

The daze of disgust and fear takes over again. Here she was, on the one hand a dynamic, bold woman pursuing MBA from a coveted institute and on the other hand she was cowering to the hollow threats of this obnoxious man, who was a bad friend at best. They had been close friends for over a year. Sapan had professed his love and when she had made it clear that she did not feel the same way, things turned sour. She even gave him a chance upon his constant insistence to meet him once, but he tried to molest her when she firmly turned down his proposal. She had just hoped this obsessive behaviour would stop after that. She expected her friend to be a decent man and give up imposing himself but he turned out to be an entitled brat. The incessant calls, the stalking, the ridiculous threats! *Is anyone keeping score of men who lose total sense of decency when they're turned down and become a monster?"* she thought to herself. At times, she couldn't believe that she was going through this and that it was Sapan, a once-upon-a-time dear friend doing this to her. She did not even know if she should take his threats of circulating her morphed images online or defaming her, seriously. She couldn't decide how to respond and specifically, if her response would blow this further out of proportion. She had just been hoping this would stop but things were getting worse. Probably for the first time in her life she didn't have any clarity on her actions.

Maya starts empathizing with women, who endure mental harassment and abuse. Such abuse clouds one's judgment, makes one vulnerable and pushes one into inaction. One is left on scraps of hope that it'll all stop miraculously one day, but does it ever stop? It all made sense to her now. Her inaction and avoidance had been prolonging her misery all along; she couldn't let this go on. The realization made her feel as if she had gotten up from a fever dream, when, like clockwork, the phone rang again. She picked up. *"Hello Maya, you cannot keep ignoring me. Please meet me, you know I truly love you. I'll do anything to get you, please talk to me"*, Sapan gets cut off by Maya at this point, *"This isn't love, Sapan. This is harassment and I am done with it. Every day I am losing my sense of self because of you. This is the last time I am talking to you and let me make it clear, if you do not stop, I'll be raising a formal complaint. So please spare us both this unpleasantness and leave me alone."* Sapan is initially taken aback at this shift of tone but he chuckles and keeps up, *"Oh Maya, please tell me what formal complaint are you going to raise? Wouldn't it complicate things for your upcoming internship in US? Stop making a fool of yourself. You know I'll make you happy so just..."* Maya is incandescent with rage, *"Listen to me carefully, you fool! You have threatened to circulate morphed images of me online and that is a cognizable offence. You've followed me on my way home, that is also a cognizable offence. I am serious when I say this is the last time you hear from me. If you pester me any further, I'm definitely going to the police. Please do not worry about my internships and such. Take this warning of mine very seriously."* Saying this, Maya hangs up. She wells up but these are tears from feeling like herself after ages. The exhaustion of the day, more so of the last hour, gets to her as she dozes of.

Maya wakes up to 4 missed calls; all of them from her team-mates. She mutters *"Oh I'm late"* as she springs out of the bed. It was a restful sleep after so long, she almost doesn't want to panic for being late. She reaches her college, pleased with how everything is coming together and is soon greeted by her team-mates, functioning in the last-day event frenzy. *"Let's take a final look at the green-room setup, shall we?"* Maya tells Payal, as they both sift through the charts. A familiar figure moves towards her from the right corner. *"Maya"*, a palpably drunk Sapan calls out; he is barely able to stay still. Maya feels a chill go down her spine but tells him firmly *"I think I told you to stop bothering…"* Sapan leaps towards her and before Maya can finish her sentence, she finds herself on the floor with seething pain on her right cheek, neck and arms. "Oh my god! "Is it acid?" "What did he do?" The screams and commotion around her fade as she loses consciousness.

Maya wakes up in a hospital, coming to terms with an altered face and an altered life. Coming to terms with the scars of spite because she spurned a man's advances. She is getting better with the love and support of her loved ones; it helps that Sapan was arrested immediately. She feels he did rob her sense of self after all! She wonders if she would have escaped this affliction had she spoken up earlier or acted sooner. It doesn't matter now. Maya is not one to wallow in self-pity. She is already working for acid attack survivors, finding strength and solidarity in empowering other women who had the same misfortune as her. She still avoids mirrors though, but she's working on it…. Maybe one day, she'll face the mirror and still feel like herself.

Why can't my mother let the country awake? – Poetry

(With apologies to Rabindranath Tagore.)

-Gaurav Julka

Where the man is without fear
and the woman is left to die;

Where giving birth to a girl child
is the most heinous crime;

Where the women are chosen
at cheaper prices than ever;

Where respect for a mother is barely pocked-sized to
your own; pristine relationships are publicly sold;

Where a wife is obliged to starve
before her man can dine;

Where an office employee is made to sleep for
promotions and a pregnant girl is left to cry;

Where the women are not allowed
to jaunt a holy shrine;

Where it seems that the God has failed
to affirm the equilibrium on earth's life;

Where millions of them suffer
and no one to probe their voice;

Into that reality of India, My Father;
This time let my 'mother let the country awake'?

Unblemished Mother India – Poetry

(With apologies to Rabindranath Tagore.)

- Maitridevi Sisodia

I yearn for a marvellous Mother India,

free from gender-bias and such traits;

Where girl children are born to meet pride and love,

not to cause any regrets,

Where every girl crosses that high-school gate

and is let to shape her days,

Where every housewife gets respect

with importance to the opinions she lays;

Where no daughter of the land is led to suicide,

out of demands in-laws' hood,

We will all unite against dowry and such devils,

succeed against them we would.

Where no daughter of the land is raped and killed,

not to the criminal's will,

We will lead out truthful judgments,

doing that the criminal mentality we kill,

Where a daughter fearlessly can set out,

no matter sun's shining or not around,

Where no man feels less for a woman

and equally understands her wound,

A land which we will truly adorn with equality,

unblemished and full of pride;

Come world, let us take you,

let us take you for an Unblemished India's ride!

Oh, I hope I live to say that and to see that,

Mother India with that stout might,

Let there be no bias against any daughter of the land,

Lord, let there be light!

My Rapist Friend – Letter/ Prose

-Gaurav Julka

Dearest Rapist,

I hope you are doing great. Of course, you are; your case is still pending in one of the inutile Indian courts. Well, don‹t worry; I don‹t care about it. After all, even ‹rapists› are entitled to human rights. I have not written this letter to abuse you or embarrass you, because I know that is technically impossible. Moreover, I am not really sure how to abuse to an abuser?

Anyways, the reason I have written this letter is to let you know that I understand your 'need' to rape. You see, I am a 'man' too. I too have needs; but I find 'peaceful solutions' to satisfy my needs rather than the ones which involve 'hard work'. Yes, hard work; all that kidnapping, tearing clothes off, strangling, controlling the noise, post implementation validation...it's just too much, you know! I know you were helpless then, because you did not have a book called 'Rape - Raping for Dummies' or '101 tips to an excellent rape' *(Btw. these books might come to the market soon)*. But don't you worry, I won't make you buy that book. I am here to give free solutions *RIGHT NOW*.

So, the next time when you are driving your SUV with a bunch of friends drunk on 'Desi Daaru' and feel like 'Raping' that innocent girl of Blah-Blah school, just because her legs are waxed and boobs are bigger; refer to this Manual.

Step 1: Check: Are you near Juhu Beach, Grant Road in Mumbai or GT Road, Delhi?

You are? Great! Go to the Juhu beach, walk along the beach for a while towards the less crowded area, you will find women with umbrellas. Yes! They will do you. Price range: 50 to 150 | Hotel Room Experience: 350-500 *(I am talking in INR)* --- It's safe. There is a police station at Juhu beach. They know about it; but don't you worry. They are 'good friends' with the women there. You can check this on Facebook Mutual friend list. Grant Road: Ah! I am sure you are already aware. Just walk down the lane, knock on the open doors, go in and the world is yours. (Delhi & Mumbai)

Step 2: Can't find one? Need better options? Too risky to look for a prostitute? If you are all set to be 'Free' from the acquisition of the first rape, I can safely assume that you are rich. Then why do desi? Go do a Tracy. Many countries have legalized prostitution -- No risk. *Btw. if you drop by Singapore, ping me.*

Step 3: Can't afford any of these?

Well, you could marry. Marriages are about two types of deals a) Dowry b) Sex. Women are anyways 'forbidden' to have sex before marriage, marriage is a good way to find someone 'nice' and 'pure' plus you get the Dowry!

Step 4: Don't want to marry?

Oh! So, you are the 'escape from the responsibility type'. Fair enough! We still have a solution; heard of Sex-toys? Porn? No? Google it, dude!

With all these solutions handy, I don't think you would need to rape again but if you do, I have a suggestion; leave alone the innocent school and college going girls. They are too young and not really fun.

Now, let's talk about the experience. Do you think you had the best sex experience ever? Nah, bullshit! A study shows a man's sexual experience increases by 45% if the woman is completely involved in the process. Well, you don't care about it...do you?

(Btw, do you feel the same? It is women who provoke us to rape, right? They wear short skirts, short tops, have long hair, dress up in school dresses and dare to WALK right next to us. Plus, we have Bollywood. It motivates the blatant objectification! Ah!)

So, we were talking about experience. I just wanted you to know that the lucky girl you raped is right now availing free medical services from a government hospital. Don't worry, she doesn't have AIDS or STD. She is just suffering from intense depression because her father committed suicide right after the auspicious day when you celebrated her rape. That actually is good news (for you) because now, that she has no financial support. You can cut-open a deal with the victim, you might have to spend some money to bribe the lawyers, media etc. but hey, it's India! It will work! *(Wait, did I just use the word Victim? My apologies!)*

I also wanted to ask you about an incident which happened with one of my friends back in the year 1999. Were you the guy who molested my friend physically when she was in Class 2? You were the one teaching her art, as well as molestation, right? And also, the guy who rubbed his crotch against my

Mumbai maid during the local train journey from Andheri to Dadar? No? Well, he must be one of those 102200 friends of yours!

Another question: Have you ever cried so much that you couldn't breathe properly?

I have seen that cry on young girls who are blemished for life. I have seen that cry in the strongest of men when their daughters commit suicide. I have seen that cry in every woman's heart, scared to leave her house at night. I have seen that cry in my country's soul where women are left to die. All of this because of people like you who ignore the sufferings and turn a blind eye.

To you, Dear Rapist; don't take this letter for granted. This letter does not signify your win; neither does it say you have changed the world for good or bad. You have destroyed lives for sure, but Life still plans to live as it used to. Don't you forget, there will always be people like us fighting against your wants and choices; standing up for the weak or rather, for the unheard and making a difference in this world.

I hope the memory of your heinous crime will always haunt your nights. May these walls you're between become smaller with time. May you realize that you are guilty of a crime and just maybe, you feel apologetic for a while?

I wish you all the best for your future endeavours.

Yours Faithfully,

A Young, Ignorant Indian Voice.

Letter to Men – Letter / Prose

- Maitridevi Sisodia

Dear Men,

We'd like to establish that feminism is not about hating men, right off the bat. Please do not associate "feminism" with extrapolated, extreme versions of the term, to dismiss it right away. If your first instinct upon hearing a woman's experience, is an urge to box it up as "radical feminism", chances are you haven't made a genuine effort to even recognize the challenges women go through because of how our society functions. We'd urge you to cross that Rubicon. If you were to be sincerely receptive of understanding the trials and tribulations women go through, you'd start feeling and acting differently. Patriarchy has been exploiting and abusing women for ages; but, throwing expletives at patriarchy achieves nothing. We're allies in furthering the goal of a fair, equal, progressive society. We need a deep cleanse of the system, a system that you and I are a part of. We need each other if we're to succeed in this mission.

When several thousand women came forward with their stories as #MeToo movement virally spread, many of you stood by them as pillars of support. But some of you started propagating the "Not All Men" narrative. Now, there is nothing wrong factually, but why does this need to be said? No woman who shares her scarring story, means to say that all men are abusive. The "Not All Men" narrative is not just unnecessary but also problematic. Say hypothetically, if you were locked in a cage with 10 snakes out of which 9 were non-venomous, you would not know which one is venomous. So the rational and wise choice would be to avoid them all. It is a similar situation, we cannot let our guard down, for we simply do not know which man turns out to abusive; and, going by the daily horrors that women face, there are plenty. So please do not push "Not All Men" narrative when a woman shares or recounts her experiences. This narrative not only belittles her experience and takes away the focus from the oppressor, it also pitches us against each other. It is not a women VS men issue; don't make it one.

Many of you are quick to point out the cases wherein women have abused the laws meant to protect them. By all means, such women should be brought to the book. No one is championing different treatment for women doing wrong. But, to hold up these isolated cases to just obliterate the overall experience of millions of women who have been at the receiving end of horrible treatment, who had their dignity stripped off, is doing a great disservice to the cause of working towards a progressive society. It's like saying that if one woman lies, it makes all women's experiences worthy of suspicion but for the several men who have committed appalling crimes on women, one must not question their credibility. Unfair! This is thinly veiled misogyny at best. Such cases do not justify projecting every woman's story as dubitable. Hundreds of us never speak up in the first place, for the fear of not being believed. This approach only pushes scores more to silence, which only emboldens the oppressive men.

For a long time, men have been able to get away with so much that now, confronted with the possibility that this might change, men feel uncomfortable. How often have we come across the "Let it slide, it was just a joke" approach? Gaslighting women by making them think that it was their interpretation of a suggestion that was wrong, is another abhorrent crutch that abusive men fall back on. This "let it slide" attitude has been a shot in the arm of men who abuse women. It has also stiffened the possibility for men who start doing that without identifying it, essentially. Please do not perpetuate this "just a joke" tactic; it only helps piggyback further abuse.

Some of you said that you felt threatened in interacting with women after the #MeToo movement sparked off. This is rather gloomy. Think of what women have endured for years, dealing with systemic abuse. And this is not a women's issue, it is a men's issue. You've made misogynistic jokes or you've laughed at them. You've pushed the boundaries, when a woman said she felt uncomfortable and covered it as a joke. You've felt that a woman owed you her body, if you've provided for her. You've called women choicest slurs, believing they deserved the tag. Now, if you claim with certainty that you have never done these acts, you've definitely witnessed them happening around you. Did you call out your friend when he made that rape joke? Did you call out your colleague who was making a woman uncomfortable? Did you speak up when you saw your friend touching a woman inappropriately on the dance floor? You might never have assaulted a woman yourself, but you still benefit from this oppressive system that holds us back. Hence, it is imperative that you take a stand. We're grateful for the few of you who do speak up and shut down such abusive behaviour. We can only attain a change when speaking up and shutting down said behaviour is made a rule and not an exception.

Please stop trivializing our ordeals. Be an ally. We need each other.

With Sincere Hope,

Women

Rosa Fanai – Short Story/ Prose

-Gaurav Julka

I

A stream of tears rolled down her eyes. She knew it; this is exactly what she had been waiting and striving for over years. With that big fat graduation hat up in the air, she was finally an IIT Delhi Graduate with Majors in Electronics & Communication.

Rosa Fanai was born in the beautiful capital city of Mizoram, Aizawl. She was more than just a normal Indian girl struggling to represent her voice; she was a fighter. Rosa's parents were Dhaba owners on the capital highway connecting Assam with Mizoram. She had always lived a life of struggle but never had whined about the same. She always made her own way by securing a scholarship to the best school in Aizawl, as well as, qualifying for the prestigious IIT JEE and securing a seat at the prestigious Indian Institute of Technology, Delhi.

Rosa was a fine scholar. Her innovations in chip computing speed enhancement had given her ownership of three IEEE papers and a placed job at the Ministry of Science & Technology, Government of India. She was assigned to work as an Engineer at the advance research lab in Delhi under the department of Electronics Research. Rosa had her dream life ahead, which would also mean an end to her struggling phase in life. She knew she had made her parents, her family proud and she knew this is just the beginning. Rosa was living in New Delhi for over four years now. She had started calling herself a Delhiite; in fact, a proud Delhiite. Even though Rosa had always faced some sort of discrimination because she was a North-East Indian, she had a positive attitude towards life and people in general. Students from her university would always try to tease her with names like 'Chinki','Firangi', 'Chini' but that never brought her morale down. In fact, it would sometimes act as her motivation to prove and do something better.

Rosa was just like any other Delhi girl; shopping, Desi ice-cream, Def Col Mocha, Chandani Chowk, and SRK movies were some of her top favourite activities in Delhi. If not doing any of these, she would always be found studying on one of the green benches in the IIT Garden or eating Chicken Momos at the Baba Momo Canteen. Rosa was bold, fun loving, hardworking and innovative; she had promised herself that she would always be like that. In three days, Rosa would step into the corporate world full of new experiences, new people and a brand-new way of living life. Rosa's life was indeed going to change. Indeed.

Rosa's first day of work was exactly how she had predicted or rather, dreamed of. She had a small cabin to herself with all basic office necessities. She had access to one of the most advanced electronic labs in India and surprisingly, the boss she was reporting to was none other than her favourite technology book writer Krishnan P Gupta. Rosa had been reading books & papers written by Krishnan since she was preparing for IIT JEE; she knew this couldn't get better.

As months passed, Rosa became the shining new star of the office. She would take up as much work as she could and also focus on her own personal research. Rosa had struck an amazing friendly relationship with all her colleagues except one; Krishnan would still never talk to her beyond work and would rarely appreciate her for her excellence. Rosa was fine by the same. She knew it was her honour to work with Mr. Krishnan. She would keep striving for excellence and would respect her idol. Beyond office hours, Rosa had a normal life. A life with few really good friends, a handsome boyfriend from Kashmir, few glasses of Margarita at the NFS colony and a beautiful government flat in GK-1. Rosa would often spend time writing letters to her parents. She would call them often too, but she always felt that writing letters made more sense.

It was Rosa's birthday; she was elegantly dressed in an awe-inspiring black dress gifted to her by Vijay, her boyfriend. Her arrival in office was greeted by a surprise birthday cake prepared by one of her Lab assistants. People in her office and lab were more than excited to celebrate Rosa's birthday as if it was a national holiday of some kind. Rosa was personally wished by almost everyone in the office; everyone except one. Krishnan had no interest whatsoever in such small happenings. Post-lunch, Krishnan asked his secretary to tell Rosa to meet him in his office at 3:00PM. Rosa knew why she was being called; she knew Krishnan has something special in store for her.

Rosa was in Krishnan's cabin exactly on time. After a brief eye contact and an angry blink of his eye lid Krishnan said,

"Is this how you dress up and come to work in a government office?"

Rosa was lost. She was not expecting a review of her clothes; she was not expecting their first personal conversation to be about the indecency of her clothes. Nervous and scared, she replied:

"Sir, I am sorry…I did not realize this dress would be considered indecent. I thought it would be okay because it was my birthday…it will never happen again."

"Ya Right! It's my birthday so I can dance naked and fire my CEO. Now GO!" Krishnan roared in a heavy sarcastic voice. Rosa had never seen Krishnan in this avatar. She was horrified, embarrassed and de-motivated. A little more of Krishnan's voice and she would have cried. Rosa literally ran back to her cabin and locked herself in embarrassment and sadness. All she could think of was her impression on her boss, her idol, her Krishnan.

Weeks passed and Rosa started ignoring her interactions with Krishnan because of embarrassment and fear. She had regained her enthusiasm towards work and office but always had this sulky feeling when she saw Krishnan. It was the last Friday of the month of March. Krishnan called Rosa to his cabin to discuss the quarterly review. After the review, Krishnan surprised Rosa by saying,

"I am really sorry for what I did on your birthday last month…I wasn't really myself that day. Sorry, I took everything out on you".

Rosa replied with supreme humility,

"It's okay sir, I understand I was not dressed properly and I made sure it never happened again. You don't have to be sorry for that sir"

"Let me take you out for a dinner today. I hope it will compensate for my anger", proposed Krishnan.

Rosa replied with hesitation," *That would not be necessary sir; it's okay".*

Even though she badly wanted to break the ice with Krishnan, she knew that the right thing to do at this moment was to reject the offer with humility.

"Come on I insist, we have to do this", pleaded Krishnan. Rosa could not reject or refuse it anymore; she knew that beyond this it won't be polite of her to not accept the offer.

"Sure sir, if you insist…Thank you", the humble Rosa spoke. Both left the office together later that evening in Krishnan's sleek, black Mercedes.

The dinner incepted a series of coffees, hangouts and more dinners between Krishnan and Rosa. By the month of May, Rosa had almost become a part of his family. She knew his wife and daughters and would often see them over informal and official dinners. Rosa was now Krishnan's official mentee and was working with him on all his projects. This was a real opportunity for Rosa to prove her talent; she contributed to every bit she could. She would often stay late nights in the office to make sure all her research papers were complete way ahead of time so that Krishnan could provide her proper feedback before she would submit them. This was the perfect work life Rosa had always desired; *the hands of her idol were over her head.*

It was one of those common early evening dinners when Krishnan would treat Rosa with cheap Delhi fast-food and talk about Rosa's family and her house in Aizawl. Krishnan suddenly proposed that they should go back to office and finish the sketch of the latest transformer integrated chip that they were working on. Rosa could have never rejected something as glittery as that. Soon both of them were back in their lab with a few bottles of Coke, few packets of chips, and a packet of cashew nuts.

While working Krishnan struck a conversation about his sex life and started talking to Rosa about how unsatisfied he was and how he had always wanted someone better in life.

"Rosa, do you know how it feels to be unsatisfied for over 10 years?" Krishnan rhetorically questioned. Rosa was already in a sort of culture shock; she had never expected Krishnan to talk to her about something like this. She was close enough to Krishnan to have dinner with his family but not close enough to consult him on his sex life.

"I won't know sir", replied the helpless shy girl.

The very next moment Krishnan and Rosa had an eye contact for a second. Rosa could feel Krishnan's eyes probing every part of her body, striping her naked in every sense and respect.

Wanting to console her idol, she inquired, *"Sir, are you okay?"*

Suddenly, within a part of a second, Krishnan was holding Rosa tight in his arms, looking straight into her eyes while stroking the hair near her ears.

"I have done so much for you; won't you do this for me?" Krishnan rhetorically claimed.

Rosa was stunned. Before she could realize what was happening, Krishnan was already all over her by pushing her back on the graphing table, kissing her lower lip passionately. Rosa wanted to stop him but there was no way she could push the heavy Krishnan from over her. Before Rosa could shout or realize that she was being forced into something she never thought of, Krishnan said,

"It won't hurt you if you do it once; please don't stop me"

Rosa lay there like a clay pot being modelled by Krishnan. She was quite for a millisecond. Then suddenly, she spoke,

"Please…"

II

Before she could complete…Krishnan's hand had penetrated the protection of her clothes and the other had taken care of her speaking capability. Soon Rosa found herself lying nude on the very table where she used to design engineering graphics for Krishnan's books and papers, helpless, quiet and exploited.

"Rosa…", whispered Krishnan.

One could feel the pain looking at Rosa's face with Krishnan's hand making it difficult for her to breathe. Rosa was being raped - that too with a mutual understanding.

Within a short period of ten minutes, Rosa was free again; bond to be in an emotional cage forever. After a while Rosa came to senses, quietly picked up her clothes from the floor, and started walking towards the other corner of the room to cover her naked body. Suddenly, she felt her head and her body hitting the wall; it was Krishnan again. And this time it was very painful. Tears ran down her eyes; she could not even open her mouth to breathe or cry. She could feel him pushing it beyond her capacity until she fainted.

Rosa woke up in pain; faint morning sunlight was penetrating the brown window pane. For a minute Rosa thought it was a nightmare. Looking around she found her torn clothes lying around and realized it wasn't. Her eyes looked for the Satan but he wasn't around. She quickly collected the scattered pieces of her clothes and covered herself again in the fear that even the empty space would rape her again. She wanted to leave the office before anyone entered; soon she left the morning and took the first rickshaw she found towards GK-1. She could not stop the tears rolling down her eyes, she wanted to be brave but that just remained as one of her farfetched desires. She felt exploited, used; raped.

Rosa didn't go to office for over a week. She sent a leave application to her HR without mentioning the reason; she was still comprehending the new reality of her life. She wanted to report the incident but knew it was of no use. It would only defame her very identity which she was trying to protect. She locked herself from any sort of communication with Vijay and started contemplating on the reasons of her existence and desire to continue living. Rosa had always been a bold girl and she knew she could still get over this instance. After all, it was only a one-time incident and no one else apart from them knew about it. She was being bold not because she was really bold but because she knew that her parents would die of pain if they heard the epilogue of her reality.

After more than two weeks Rosa decided to face her worse fears; she decided to join her office again. Not for the sake of her self-respect but for the sake of her parents, family and identity. She was obviously questioned by almost everyone on her absence; she gave an excuse of being sick and down with jaundice. For the first three days she had no conversation, no eye contact with Krishnan...she didn't even know if he still was working in the same office; she never had the guts to validate that. On the fourth day morning, she had her first eye contact with Krishnan. She could feel his eyes still undressing her and enjoying the pleasure of her presence. She quietly walked away without giving him a second look. Later in the day, Krishnan asked for Rosa to meet her in the office. Rosa had no options but to adhere the command of her senior. The interaction was shocking; Krishnan only talked about work, there wasn't a smallest hesitation of any sorts while he was assigning her work. All Rosa could do was keep her eyes down and listen to whatever he had to say.

The same Friday evening Rosa was forced to stay back in the office and complete her work. Even though she wanted to be home before the last ray of sunlight disappeared, that was not possible. She was still busy with the work assigned to her by Krishnan. At least she was assured that she was safe as she assumed Krishnan had left the office for good. Krishnan did leave the office but was back; he had given Rosa additional work for a reason.

Suddenly, Rosa realized a pair of scary eyes staring at her through the lab door. Before she could react, Krishnan was standing right next to her, holding her hair with his hand and making sure she was unable to shout. He whispered,

"Rosa…that was the best I ever had. If you can do it once with me and be okay with it, I think you would want me to do it again and again…I think we can come to some sort of understanding here. I don't you want to get fired and go back home defamed because you sold yourself to me for exchange of a job promotion… I want you to work in this office with pleasure" Rosa could feel Krishnan's hands penetrating her sacred spot as he said that.

Before Rosa could comprehend what Krishnan had said, she found herself again on the same table half nude. Krishnan gave complete permission to Rosa to make as much noise as possible by removing his hand from her mouth. Rosa begged for forgiveness, she begged to him to let her go, she begged him not to destroy her life but Krishnan was already inside her.

"There is no point of shouting, crying and not coming to office…this is going to be your reality from tomorrow unless you want to be on the first page of the national news and known all over India for your superb 'being whore skills'" Krishnan whispered in her ears as he finished zipping up his pants.

Rosa realized the depth of what he had said and without a tear in her eyes she stood up from the table, collected her clothes and started walking away from the lab towards her cabin.

Rosa now had a new life; the one she had never thought about in the weirdest of her dreams. She would go to office regularly just like any other employee but end up providing some sort of special services to Krishnan. Krishnan starting recording their interactions in the form of pictures and videos and soon Rosa was a keep to her boss, Krishnan. This went on for weeks; Rosa didn't mention anything about it to Vijay or to her parents. Telling her employees was a far-flung thought. She even started documenting her experiences in a diary, just to vent out what she faced in the entire day. Most of her sexual interactions with Krishnan would be lifeless as she would lie naked on the table or in his Mercedes and not feel anything; while some others were painful. Krishnan soon started calling her and refereeing to her as his slut or keep. There were even instances where Rosa had dinner with his family and later, on the pretext of dropping Rosa home, Krishnan would do her in some secluded area of Delhi.

There were times where Rosa thought about killing herself or leaving Delhi forever but whenever she did that, the picture of her parents, her family, her city and Vijay would flash by her eyes. She had somehow managed to not give Vijay any hint of what was happening with her in the office.

Rosa accepted her life. Rosa accepted the reality of her being a keep. Rosa accepted that she was born to be used.

III

With time, there was a decrease in the sheer number of sexual interactions that Rosa and Krishnan had but still, every time Rosa saw Krishnan, she would feel disgusted of her very existence. They had stop working together on almost all the projects as most of the time Krishnan would be busy satisfying his own needs.

It was the last Friday of July and Krishnan wanted to take Rosa out for a dinner date. Rosa accepted the offer fearing she anyways had no options. Krishnan had booked a table for two in one of the most expensive hotels in Delhi.

"So, you are happy right?" Krishnan said, gulping a huge piece of chicken.

"With?", Rosa replied with no interest whatsoever.

"Happy about being my keep! You always wanted to be close to me…always wanted me to give you more attention and of course, work with me" Krishnan boasted.

Rosa could only reply to that statement with a tear in her eye.

"Stop crying. You act as if you are an Indian girl who is all cultured and respectful. You don't even belong to our sect … you are more like Chinese people…People like you are good for nothing other than sex…am I right? Hahaha, he says I am right" Krishnan roared looking down towards his pants.

"Krishnan…" said Rosa after digesting what he really meant.

"Don't forget you are still supposed to call me as 'Sir'", Krishnan boasted finishing his last sip of wine. More tears rolled down Rosa's face. The only thought she had in her mind was 'why couldn't she end her life right now?'.

"Okay, stop whining. I have booked a room in this hotel under anonymous names. Today we shall enjoy in the classic style...I think you should stop this Electronics and Communication madness of yours and become a full-time slut...I might be able to find you few customers... Hahaha, you must also be wanting diversity, right? Haha" Krishnan said as he laughed away to glory.

As Rosa and Krishnan entered the room, Rosa requested for a wine bottle before they could proceed.

"So now Rosa wants to be romantic, eh?" Krishnan rhetorically questioned and ordered wine through room service. Soon, the wine was served. Rosa drank an entire glass in one go and asked for more. She did the same with the next four glasses.

Krishnan started to undress her. Rosa too joined in undressing Krishnan. Seconds later, with slightest of any sort of hesitation, Rosa stabbed the glass of wine right through Krishnan's stomach. She grabbed the other glass and penetrated it right through his groin. Suddenly, everything was peaceful again.

Rosa grabbed everything she thought that was hers, some money from Krishnan's wallet and ran towards the exit of the hotel with a sense of accomplishment along with some sense of peace. Even though in pieces, she could now at least look herself in the eye. The same night, Rosa transferred all her savings and the money she had into her parents' accounts, left a letter for Vijay to not seek her anymore and embarked a new journey in life. With the little money that she was left with, she bought some rat poison from the local grocery store, a pair of scissors, a knife, a packet of cashew nuts and a small cup of Vanilla ice-cream.

She boarded the first interstate public bus she could find. Eating her flavoured ice-cream with cashew nuts, Rosa was finally at peace.

(To be continued in future works of the author)

A Dark Aubade – Aubade/ Poetry

-Gaurav Julka

Ting Ring Ting!
The strings of the gloomy guitar sings,
Halt your horses; untie those lustrous strings.

It's the time,
thy sunset of hope brings aurora
of darkness to the rings.
Shiny lights rise and shine...
Welcome to the Sin City crime.
Daylight has concluded;
so, has the Colorado Springs
I hope you're prepared;
ahead you have a rapid climb.

Don't try to fly, or you will die
they won't spare your water wings.

Ting Ring Ting!
The strings of the gloomy guitar sings,
Halt your horses; untie those lustrous strings.

It's the time,
of celebration at nine;
get ready with your suicidal slings
the dancers are in; but they are part-time
It's you. Urged to complete the prime.
Sell yourself, to the Lord and to the kings;
Such is life; every night it shall rhyme.

Don't try to cry coz' no one will buy
If not here, they would sell you at Beijing's.

Ting Ring Ting!
The strings of the gloomy guitar sings.

What's wrong with her? - Poetry

-Maitridevi Sisodia

Dressed up to the nines,

Sipping on fine wine,

No male chaperone by her side

What's wrong with her?

Mother of two,

With a husband well-to-do,

She wants a superfluous career still,

What's wrong with her?

A duty-bound wife,

Seeking separation for life,

For she feels "harassed" by her husband,

What's wrong with her?

Living life on her terms,

Disregarding the society's whines.

Trying to break the patriarchal mould,

What's wrong with her?

Every woman, who has ever taken a stand cannot
but hear this enough,

What's wrong with her? What's wrong with her?

Is Justice all but a privilege? - Poetry

-Maitridevi Sisodia

Is Justice all but a privilege?

Driven back and forth,

To adjust the affluent edge,

Who should I loathe?

Is Justice all but a privilege?

Is it wrong to be right?

For the pen lies to the page

I wish I could just rage,

Is Justice all but a privilege?

Oh, can you wipe their tears,

For the Satan might be named a Sage,

Shallow are these waters, never clear!

Why do we keep failing our daughters? - Prose

-Maitridevi Sisodia

Nirbhaya. Priyanka. Asifa. Manisha. These are just a few names that spark the ghastly memories of horrendous crimes. These bloodcurdling cases came to light and turned into movements. Hundreds of thousands of Indians participated in candle marches and protested these abominable crimes against women. In every new protest, sleep the forgotten memories of several women who are subjected to this heinous crime. These forgotten memories lie dormant - in the cracking yellow pages of abandoned files, in the ashes of the victim's body, in the tears of the victim's family and sometimes in the nightmares of the survivor. India reports about 88 rape cases a day. 88 lives, being set up every day for a lifetime of trauma, if they survive. These are just the reported numbers, which indicates the reality is much more wretched. Sexual crimes against women have been steadily on the rise. Rape-culture is a loathsome reality and a raging social tragedy.

The practice of victim-shaming and victim-blaming is as pervasive as these sexual crimes against women. Whenever a case comes to light, our first instinct is to wonder about the whereabouts of the victim, or the inappropriate time for them to be out of the house, or why they were alone. Catcalling, molestation, groping, sexual crimes. It is endless. The burden to stay safe is placed on women. Mothers become frantic until daughters get back home. Friends keep checking up on women till they get back home safe. Just the act of being out and about, requires a woman to come armed with pepper spray, whistles and what not. The amount of mental trauma that women go through for simplest things such as getting home safe, is unnerving and unjust. It is easier for a man to stab and kill his wife, in full public view – like in the unfortunate incident that happened in Delhi recently - than for a woman to not get into trouble. What a repulsive reality!

In the hinterlands, where lot of cases might go unreported, sexual crimes against women are not just intended to brutalize the individual woman, but to rob the honour of the community. A family's and community's honour is reposed in the chastity of their female members. We often come across news where land disputes result in women being raped. Women's bodies become collateral damage to men's clashes. We are a modern civilization but somehow these abhorrent medieval practices live on.

Society teaches women to sweep their discomfort under the carpet, this builds on & on. Soon enough, women learn to start sweeping trauma under the carpet too. Many girls experience molestation or harassment early on; some don't even understand it. The ones who do, feel very ashamed; they feel as if it was their fault and so, they choose not to speak up. Most unfortunate for some, when they choose to tell their loved ones about their troubles, they are shushed for the fear of bringing humiliation to the family. Imagine what they grow up believing! We're a generation of women who have grown up in a society that teaches us to shut up about our discomfort and trauma, to feel humiliated for it.

We vilify and slander women who lead, regardless of the level they lead at. We are inherently vicious to strong women. Obnoxious rumours about them are commonplace. This stands true for a woman who leads a small sales team, to a woman who's running the state or country, perhaps. The ad-hominem attack on a woman always begins with them being unworthy, moving on to how they reached a certain position via dubious or salacious means. The tendency to prove successful/thriving women to be unworthy, is deeply cemented, despicably so. Try thinking how many times you've come across this yourself. I can bank on the fact that all of us, regardless of profession and age, have at some point been witness to this contemptible tendency.

We have strong laws against rape in our country; but, the solution doesn't lie in having strong laws. Just strong laws don't play deterrent, it is the strong, timely implementation of these laws that would be a deterrent. There need to be reforms to fix gaps in reporting and registering these crimes. It should be our aim to not let any crime go unreported or unregistered. Focus has to be on prompt investigation, while putting in place survivor-support mechanisms.

We will keep failing our daughters until we, as a society, stop with victim-shaming and victim-blaming; until men change their behaviour; until the oppressors are punished without unreasonable delay; until we stop denigrating women. Till all this happens, we cannot overcome this toxic culture. Raising the next generation of men to respect women and to be aware of women's life experiences will help us get there. We cannot address the violent and sexual crimes against women without addressing the men committing them. Let's put the collective shame of a crime on the criminal. Let the loafers who feel they can get away with cat-calling or eve-teasing be dealt sternly. Let the stalkers who make life a living hell for women receive prompt response from law enforcement agencies. Let the rapists who think they can get away with atrocious crimes against women, be subjected to swift sentencing. Let us strive for a country where a mother doesn't have to worry about her daughter reaching home safe, where a father doesn't need to compromise his daughter's education for the fear of her safety in a different city, where a rape survivor is not shamed by the society and the system, where the law of the land is strongly implemented.

Outrageous sexual crimes and rape cases occur almost every single day, few manage to spark serious conversations and rare few end up becoming movements. While these movements are short-lived, we must ensure that the resolve to fight this doesn't fizzle alongside the movement. We do not agitate enough as a people, as a system. Day after day, petrifying horrors come to light; these are, but a fraction of tragedies that really occur. These several other tragedies don't spark outrage; they don't evoke protests because, they're silenced and swept under the carpet. We need not be silenced. We need to relentlessly agitate at a personal level, and at a social level. Only then can we hope to change this repulsive culture that has set like an indelible stain on our social fabric. Let us break this vicious cycle. Let them not remain simply a statistic!

Power Immense – Poetry

- Maitridevi Sisodia

In those hands rests power immense,

The hands that rocked your cradle;

And that she is feeble is just your stance,

Why can't you feel that?, Tis no riddle.

In those hands rests power immense,

The hands that help your hand, helped you walk,

All they deserve is respect and love, but in vain,

When those hands are in need, you'll not fail to balk;

In those hands rests power immense,

The hands that held the kitchen knives,

Have taken care of you in all sense,

And still you say, worthless are their lives?

In those hands rests power immense,

The hands that taught you the way of life,

At every turn, every step, on this road so dense,

Yet you say she's weak. Shame that thought is rife.

Tell me simply - Poetry

- Maitridevi Sisodia

Tell me simply,

If you see rude men

Cat-calling a woman,

Then you'll raise your voice.

Tell me simply,

If you spot a woman

In certain trouble,

Then you'll rush to help.

Tell me simply,

If you saw a woman

Beaten and stabbed on the street,

Then you won't be a bystander but intervene.

We mourn and mourn,

The many bruises. The many losses,

But mourning isn't enough,

So, tell me simply, that I can count on you.

Fragrance of Defiance
– Short Story

- Maitridevi Sisodia

I

Chanda is over the moon about her new books, she has been going through them all day. Her brother and other neighbourhood kids are out playing, calling for her, but she wants to flip through her new books. It's early winter evening; darkness descends on the horizon. She gets a candle and continues going through her books. Her mother smiles and looks on, as she prepares chapatis for dinner. Her brother, who has just gotten back from playing, mocks her saying, *"Oh, what're you going to do reading these books all day? Will you become a teacher? Go help Maa with dinner."* Proud Chanda holds her head high and says *"You'll see, I'll study and become a Memsahib"*. Her mother smiles at her daughter's grit. Her brother snatches her books playfully and runs across the small room.

Chanda is irked, *"Quit it! Give it to me, give my book back to me"*.

"Chanda! Get up, our stop is in 5 minutes". Half asleep, she keeps mumbling, *"Give it back to me"*, Chanda opens her eyes. *"It was that dream, again"*, she says to herself. Neelam asks her with concern. *"Are you alright? Bad dream?"* Chanda gives half a smile and replies, *"I am alright, thanks for letting me nap, I know how much you love talking my ear off. This must have been quite the sacrifice"*. Neelam chuckles, *"You bet, you're buying me imli on our way back in the evening"*. The train stops; a sea of people get off and a sea of people get in. Chanda and Neelam are among the several maids getting to their workplaces on this balmy Mumbai morning. *"Just a dream"*, Chanda thought to herself again, as they hurried towards the bus that'd get them to Powai. It was one of those dreams, she had often; perhaps it was a peek in her past. She always wanted to study and become a teacher, but here she is, hurrying to serve her Memsahibs. She asked Neelam why Kamla didn't join them today. Neelam grimaced, *"Her husband beat her up badly last night, yet again. She has a broken arm and bruises all over. I feel so bad for her, why does God do this? At least our husbands don't beat us that often or that bad. Her husband treats her worse than an animal and now she cannot even threaten him with a police complaint"*. Two months ago, Kamla tried to

register a complaint, but instead got molested at the *thana*. A constable who knew her husband tipped him off, which resulted in more relentless beating.

Chanda sighed What a terrible life! She is briefly transported to the times when Ramesh was a good and responsible man. She got married to him soon after completing 12th grade. Her father passed away and it was difficult for her mother, so she agreed to get Chanda married even when she wished to study more. It's a dream that still haunts her. Initially Ramesh supported her, even appreciated the fact that she was more educated. But that bliss was short-lived; soon he turned to drinking and gambling. Now he worked odd jobs whenever he felt like and if Chanda criticized his vices, he didn't hesitate to get violent. She is grateful for the fact that because of Ramesh, she could move out of her village in Karnataka and come to Mumbai. Chanda shoulders the major responsibility of looking after Ramesh and their daughter, Rani. She didn't want to imagine the daily trials she would have had to endure for birthing a daughter, if they were still living in the village. Rani is her glimmer of hope in an otherwise morose life. Ensuring good education and a good life for her, is the mission of Chanda's life. Despite the stress and difficulties, Chanda goes about her life with a bright smile. A smile so deceptive, one might even think she was genuinely happy.

Both of them get off the bus. Neelam sprints on, saying *"See you at the bus-stop at 4"*. Chanda nods. She has taken up more work. She cooks at a few houses, cleans at a few houses, and does both at some houses. She even takes up embroidery and stitching jobs in the little time she has left. It is laborious, but it ensures she has enough to look after her family and her daughter's education. Rani is a sharp and enthusiastic student, just as Chanda was when she was younger. She has been trying to get her admitted to a reputed, private school under the weaker sections' quota. Rani didn't make it to that list, which came out last week. Ramesh tells her it is a futile exercise and nothing would come of it but Chanda still has hope. After all, that's the sole mission of her life currently. The only thing that drives her.

Clouded by all these thoughts, Chanda rings the doorbell. Geeta opens the door, and greets her with the biggest smile, *"I've been waiting for you so eagerly"*. Geeta had been helping her with Rani's admission to the private school, since last year. Chanda smiles back and says, "Didi, *I know today is your cheat-day, I'll get to preparing the halwa right away"*. Geeta cracked up and replied, *"It's not that, silly! You'll be making the halwa but for a different reason. Yesterday evening, the school posted its second list, Rani has been selected for admission to 3rd grade."* For a few moments, Chanda couldn't even process this information; she gasped. Still not able to believe it, she said, *"But didn't they say we had to apply next year again, Didi?"* Geeta pulled off a paper, showing her the letter about the second list and explaining it to her. Chanda is ecstatic. She barely contains herself from jumping and screaming with joy. She feels like the world has changed for her in that moment. She pulls out her small cell-phone, tied in her handkerchief, to call Ramesh. She's so pumped, even the faulty buttons don't irk her right now. *"Hello, I've great news. Rani got into the private school"*, Chanda says with a big smile. *"Hmm, Okuy, we'll see"*, Ramesh mutters from the other side. He's drunk already and indifferent about this, but Chanda didn't want to dampen her joy today. She floats in happiness that day, finishing her work, one house to another.

II

Chanda meets Neelam at the bus-stop, hugging her as she informs her about Rani's admission. Neelam equally gushes, *"I am so happy for you, Chanda. Rani is a bright girl; she will make something for herself. You better continue helping our kids with their studies, even if Rani goes to different school."* Chanda nods and laughs, *"Of course silly, I won't stop helping. Now let's hurry, I want to go to a temple today."* They reach the station, and luckily get a fast train back. Chanda is in a happy daze, looking at the women sharply dressed in formals, she almost sees a grown-up Rani among them. Life would be so much better and different for her. Their station arrives. Ah! time just flies when one is happy, she thinks. Usually, she feels tired by the time they get back, but today she feels like she has just woken up from a restful sleep, so refreshed. Brisking up her pace, she picks up sweets while walking back home. She is stopped in her track, at the sight of beautiful flowers and gajras, at the small flower stall near the temple. She always loved gajras; today deserves one, she thinks. She buys some flowers to offer at the temple and a beautiful gajra made of fresh roses and mogra, for herself.

She goes to Nirmala Amma's place near her shanty, to get Rani. Amma looks after the children from neighbouring shanties, till their mothers get back. She gives her sweets, thanks her. Rani is chuffed upon learning about this and jumps with joy, *"Maa, I'm going to learn so much. People say they've different teachers for different subjects in that school and they give great lessons."* Rani has been studying in the government school close by. Even her teacher has been telling Chanda how brilliant Rani is and she could do really well with a better school. Rani is over the moon. Chanda plants a kiss on her cheek and tells her that she's going to prepare a feast for dinner to celebrate today.

It is late night. Ramesh has still not come back. Rani went to sleep at 10, waiting for her father to share her happiness. Ramesh comes back at 11, reeking of alcohol and in a bad mood. He had lost money, once again. Chanda, desperate to let today pass without any ugliness, chooses not to say anything. She greets him with a smile and says, *"Rani waited for you, she just went to sleep. She'll go to that big school from new term now. I've prepared your favourite kheer, come let's eat"*. Ramesh looks at her and asks *"Why are you wearing this gajra, huh?"* Chanda is a bit taken aback but tells him that she had been to the temple to pray upon this happy news. Ramesh scowls with anger, *"What happy news? Even without the fees, there would be more expenses at that school. We cannot afford that. Stop all this nonsense"*. Pouring kheer for him, Chanda quips, *"Well, if we can afford to keep losing money to gambling, we can afford to send her to a better school. You don't worry about it."* Ramesh turns red with rage at this point and smacks her across the face. Her joy turns to ashes, for she can sense what's to come. He beats her black & blue, that night. Pulling out the gajra in her hair, he yells, "*You common whore! Gajra, huh? You don't need me to worry about money, huh? You don't think I understand all this.*" Chanda cries and folds her hands. All the while, enduring the beating, she's just keeps praying that Rani shouldn't get up to see this. Chanda feels like howling but doesn't even let a sob out. Ramesh forces himself on her after the beating and whispers in her ear, "*You better give me a son, soon.*"

Something breaks inside Chanda. She collectively feels the pain she had confined to a corner in her heart, of having an alcoholic, thankless husband… she feels the weight of all her unfulfilled dreams. She starts wondering what she did wrong. She had been a good wife, even when Ramesh's behaviour kept getting worse. She kept ignoring his drinking and gambling habit and kept working harder for her family. What if Rani ends up like her a few years from now? The mere thought of it sends a chill down her spine. She cannot let that happen to her daughter; tears rolled down her cheek. She couldn't sleep all night; she made a vow to herself to not let her daughter's education and security be threatened by Ramesh's addictions. She did not quite know what she was going to do, but she had a steely resolve to get herself out of the situation. It was an unusual feeling. She felt vulnerable but at the same time she was feeling this incredible strength. She felt totally powerless and mighty powerful, in the same breath. It was strange because she felt like her world was falling apart, but she also knew she was going to build a better one. Fluctuating between these extremes, Chanda dozes off around dawn.

Few months later...

Chanda is hurrying Rani to her school-bus. *"It is time, Rani. Finish your milk"*, she says as she zips her school-bag. She takes Rani and scampers towards the bus. She smiles and waves as the bus leaves. She has a long day ahead but this joy will keep her going. She meets Kamla, as she rushes back. *"Haven't you left for work? Here, I brought you some bananas"*, Kamla says catching her on the way. Chanda helped Kamla move to a working women's shelter, a month after she started living there herself. It is not much, but it gives them safe space and helps them get on their feet, till they are ready to move out. *"I'm going in the noon today. There are some places for rent close to Rani's school that I'm going to see now and later an evening course that Saumya Didi here told me about. I can study and become a teacher, Kamla. Come along if you can"*, she tells her with a smile. Kamla nods and replies, *"...and stop bringing things for me, I'll come to relish the puranpoli you make after we find you work"*. Kamla has tears in her eyes, *"You're so brave, I can never thank you enough, and I'd have never left that life in hell without your help"*. Chanda blinks back tears as she consoles Kamla. *"Now let's hurry, we'll find some tea on the way to the station"*, she says. Chanda buys two small roses from the flower stall at the station, gives one to Kamla. Kamla eyes her curiously and says, *"So now, you wear one every day, is it?"*. Chanda grins, as she smells the fragrant rose and fixes it in her bun saying, *"Yes. Every day, this fragile flower reminds me I've to be strong"*. It is her token of defiance and liberation. Proud Chanda walks on. Ah, sweet fragrance of defiance!

Inexhaustible rain - Free Sonnet

- Maitridevi Sisodia

The mist gathered

Veiling the view,

Just a prink shy

Of thunder's cue.

Grey clouds obscuring

The day's mirage,

Advent of the downpour

the fog's entourage.

An inexhaustible rain

Rested in those skies,

In the tutelage

Of the lashes of her eyes.

Yet the worldly woes forged on,

Drying the rains for the Time's mourn.

Where are we safe? - Poetry

- Maitridevi Sisodia

Not in the womb, not in the cradle;

Nor at school, neither in a shrine,

Home, one'd think; that should be a haven,

Alas! For some, it's a wretched prison.

Abused in marriage, 'tis all acceptable,

Spinster or widowed, that is no better,

For far too many, mere objects of pleasure,

To be overpowered at will and scatter,

Not safe in the dusk of life either,

For the sickness of mind knows no bound,

End is the sole confine and thankfully,

the death is cold. Lest the graves be ravaged, too.

Blooming Roses - Poetry

- Maitridevi Sisodia

Swaying to the spring breeze's tune,

Look at those waltzing roses in full bloom;

Oh, what warm delight they bring,

To our fragile, mortal whim.

All of them alluring, luscious and scarlet,

A floral army descended on a green carpet,

Some fuller, some leaner, some more crimson,

Some with a few withering petals, charms ever risen.

Do you think this rose could use some more petals?

Do you feel due to that one's fader tone,
the sight unsettles?

Do you wonder if that rose
would bring more joy if brighter?

Never! You admire each one of them,
and all of them altogether.

145

Darling, our bodies are like these roses on this Eden,

Thriving in one's true splendour and magnificence,

In the same glance, that you adore these blooms,

Won't you now look at yourself too?

Gender gap in learning, earning and living – Essay

- Maitridevi Sisodia

Young Asha helping her mother with the chapatis, is seemingly lost. Her mother looks at her and exclaims, "For how long are you going to wear that long face, Ashu? It has been a month now". Asha waves her hands in a frenzy of rage, "Why won't you let me continue schooling? I don't have to drop out just because our village school doesn't offer education beyond 5th grade. I can go with Bhaiya to the school across the village, you know that." Tears come rolling down her cheeks, as she covers her face. Her mother tries to hold her and says, "It is settled; you've studied enough to read. It is not safe to send you so far, my child. Nothing is going to come off it".

There are a million such Ashas with similar stories, in our country. Girls who had to drop out of school against their wishes, their futures held hostage by myriad socio-economic reasons. The effect can be observed in the literacy rate from 2011 census – for women it is **65.46%** as against **82.14%** for men. The hurdles keep increasing with higher education and age.

The Annual Status of Education Report (ASER) conducted by the NGO Pratham focuses on the age-group of 14–18-year-old school goers. One of the key findings of this report is that the **enrolment gap** between males and females in formal education system **increases with age**. There is negligible difference between boys' and girls' enrolment at age 14, but the gender gap increases widely with increasing age.

The reason for girls dropping out from schools is rooted in some social stigmas, apart from the problem of access of public schools for secondary and costlier private education. Families seem to think that the monetary and temporal resources spent on a girl child's education are wasted because of her limited earning potential. Girls are married at a younger age compared to boys, so there is inherent convention of expecting girls to take care of domestic chores from an early age.

Another concern which stifles chances of more girls attending higher classes, is the concern for their safety. Recent unfortunate events of girls being molested at school have brought this problem to the fore once again. Despite sterner legal provisions in form of POCSO (Protection of Children from Sexual Offences) act, the problem perpetrates. There have been reports which indicate that girls prefer hiding the problem for the fear of having to drop out. This is just heart-wrenching, and shows the failing of both our legal system and our society.

The All India Survey on Higher Education (AISHE), conducted by Ministry of Human Resource Development, conducts survey of students (18-23 years age group) enrolled in under-graduate, post-graduate and research-level institutes within India. AISHE has shown that India has improved in terms of gender parity in higher education, i.e., number of females enrolling as against the number of males is improving. This is a heartening static but one that unfortunately doesn't follow through its promise.

More females opting for higher education should also reflect with increased female workforce participation and consequently more women getting financially independent. However, that is not the case for India. On the contrary, female labour force participation has dropped in the last decade despite an increase in female education levels. Global average of female labour work force participation is 50%; for our East Asian neighbours it is 63%, whereas we stand at a dismal 27%.

Slew of social and infrastructural reasons are to blame for this Indian anomaly. Societal pressure for early marriage is one of the major reasons for lesser female presence in work places. As per the 2011 census, median age of marriage for women stands at 19.2 years. Most women are expected to take care of household chores and look after the family after marriage.

In many cases where married women are likely to take up jobs, problems like lack of safe modes of travel and insensitive work culture mar their prospects. Women need to be adequately protected from sexual harassment at work - a nuisance which causes a lot of women to leave their jobs. Safety at work and safe modes of commute are indispensable for more women to join work force. Additionally, society needs to transform where looking after family is not treated solely as a woman's responsibility. But, until that is achieved, work places shall have to be more sensitive to women's role in the household. Measures like flexible working hours and work from home option (where it is possible) have proven to be beneficial. It is necessary to have more women leaders on board in public and private organizations, to address these issues.

As per some studies, the International Monetary Fund's estimates indicated that if India was to achieve gender parity in work force, it would increase the GDP by a **whopping 27%**. Needless to say, that, better women work force participation would not only help evolve our society but prove to be major boost for our country's economic standing. In simple terms, empowerment of women is synonymous to empowerment of our nation.

Another area in which gender disparity holds us back is the **pay gap** - a ubiquitous problem faced world-wide. Gender pay gap in India is narrowing but still remains at 20% as per some studies. But, the gap widens, peaking at 25% for those with 11 years or more experience. This indicates how the system is skewed against women with longer career spans. In informal sector, which employs more than 80% of India's labour force, the situation would be more adverse.

Despite these constraints, many women have gone on to shatter the barriers and do exceptionally well. We have seen formidable women at leading positions in top companies, banks and even governments. But they're mostly seen as **outliers**, as exceptions not the rule. Nonetheless, these icons provide inspiration to the masses of women who're still handicapped by a system skewed against them. As a society, we must relent to achieve a stage where a woman can prosper in any which way she chooses, with her own free will. It should be a rule, not an exception.

God's Accomplice - Poetry

- Maitridevi Sisodia

As flimsy as a

Bud of rose, in full bloom,

Yet as robust as a

Diamond, cutting through all doom.

When she hauls and weeps,

Melancholy itself left disconcerted,

Yet when she fiercely roars,

The king of beasts stands appalled.

Embodiment of everything virtuous she is,

But abundantly vicious when tried,

God's own accomplice she bears

The power to nourish life.

The human cohort with a sacred craft,

Bow to the divinity that is her.

Quest for an equal world: Fighting socio-cultural norms - Prose

- Maitridevi Sisodia

Gender-neutral. Gender-equal. These have been buzzwords since the turn of the century. There has been an increasing awareness of the ever-present gender-toll, the additional barriers faced by women. There is an acknowledgment for the need of action to set it right; to be fair, regardless of gender. While some progress has been made to this effect, we're a long way off from achieving equality for women, be it in private spaces or public spaces, at homes or at workplaces.

There are multiple socio-cultural factors at play which hinder the realization of a world that doesn't hold women back. Most of these socio-cultural factors are hurdles in a woman's life, the weight of which is felt right from an early age. The hard-set patriarchal way of life reinforces this at every life-stage. Most women don't even identify or question the gross inequality that they're subjected to, because they've grown up seeing such behaviour as acceptable and natural. Much like a bird born in a cage doesn't realize it is captive and doesn't know what free flight feels like, due to the unfortunate social conditioning many women never truly realize their potential and accept playing the second fiddle. Socio-cultural norms are invisible, yet ever-present fences in a woman's life experience.

Gender roles get imposed on young girls' psyche, at an impressionable age. The household and domestic chores are widely associated with women, while the decision-making roles are associated with men, even in dual-earner households. Even today, women do 75% of the world's unpaid care work. We teach our young girls to sit a certain way, to talk in a certain tone and to walk with a certain gait. By the time young girls reach a schooling age, many of these limitations have already been absorbed by them, whittling down their true potential.

As they reach adolescence, several young girls face menstrual taboos. Taboos as absurd as "...bees will forsake their hives if touched by a menstruous woman", have been held against menstruating women from times of Pliny, the Elder (1st Century BC).

Young girls still miss school days, go through unsafe isolation practices, and lack wide access to hygienic products during their menstruation. Menstrual huts or "Chhaupadis" are still prevalent in few states in India and Nepal. The practice is rooted in the belief that a menstruating woman is unclean, impure and untouchable. These huts are usually dilapidated, with no ventilation or sanitation facilities. Women have died due to dehydration, suffocation, smoke inhalation, snake bites, etc. while living in such huts. This practice is illegal in some places, but it continues unfortunately even today. Just a couple of years ago, grim news of a woman in Nepal dying due to suffocation from a fire she lit to stay warm in a Chhaupadi, came to light. In absence of these huts, women are made to sleep outside the house or in the animal shelters. It is commonplace to have urban Indian families that don't practice this extreme isolation, forbidding menstruating women from entering kitchen, touching food or offering prayers.

A sense of impurity during menstruation, is inculcated within girls. The very indication of ability to bring life is attached with the notion of being dirty, something to be hidden and be ashamed of. No wonder, girls feel the need to hide sanitary napkins or tampons, purchase them discreetly, as if they were contraband. We must all shoulder the responsibility of undoing this sense of shame around menstruation and end regressive practices of banishing women for bleeding.

The pressure of conforming to social roles is so intense for women, that it seems as if their lives revolve around marriage and motherhood. Girls are forced to learn household chores at an early age, not because they're important and necessary life skills, but because they need to ace them to find a good suitor. The careers of young women are seen to be of ancillary importance, marriage at a suitable age being the key priority; suitability dictated by society, of course. For society, a woman's identity is incomplete until she's unmarried. "Compromise and adjust"- if you're a woman, you cannot hear this enough. Women are castigated for having high standards; it's something we have all observed at some level when it comes to finding partners, women are advised to "compromise and adjust", lest they end up alone! Women in our country would either have had this experience or if they were luckier, witnessed it happening from close quarters. It is inherently problematic that so many women have to go through this. This despicably leads to several women choosing unhappiness for a lifetime rather than choosing not to conform.

"...her wings are cut and then she is blamed for not knowing how to fly." — Simone de Beauvoir

Woefully, these words ring true after Beauvoir wrote them in her feminism treatise, "The Second Sex", over seven decades ago. Women are so whittled down by the society, that most see themselves as "the second sex", secondary to men, even in this day and age. Some studies indicate that over 70% of married women in India are still housewives. Majority of women are not allowed to choose their career. It is expected of them to give up their careers and financial independence, to take care of the household responsibilities. Women working was looked upon as pin-money, not so long ago. The notion that men should have the jobs, women working was just something that they do additionally to their primary roles as mothers or wives is still very much rooted in the social psyche. Women consider themselves fortunate if their husbands "allow" them to work; that is the testimony to how ingrained the "second sex" role is. Thousands of women give up lifelong dreams and aspirations, in many cases unwillingly, due to lack of family support. "Bad mother, bad wife" taboo still continues to be associated with ambitious women, which is nothing short of an assault on a woman's identity. There is a general scornful attitude towards ambitious, successful women, which just showcases our rotten social conditioning. Have you ever come across such reprehensible taboos for an ambitious man? Such taboos are but fences to limit women, to keep them under control.

Many working women feel doubly penalized with constant guilt for not fulfilling all their domestic duties at home and with being assumed inadequate at work owing to their family responsibility. Working women face additional pressure to perform and even then, they're denied equal advancement opportunities, as many studies have shown. Things are especially gruelling for women looking to re-enter the work-force after motherhood. Stigma is like shadow in a woman's life, it is ever-present. If a woman deviates or crosses over these glass fences i.e., social norms, she'll be vilified, regardless of whether she has chosen to be single, married, separated, divorced or widowed. This is the most parochial, yet most permissive facet of this patriarchal society. It is because a woman's identity isn't taken as a whole; it is a subset of a male in their lives. Most striking illustration of this is how broken marriages become ongoing judgment sentences on women, regardless of the circumstances. Even powerful women like MacKenzie Scott or Melinda French in progressive Western society couldn't escape the misogynistic jokes. Closer home, due to social stigma, lack of financial independence or both, many women choose to spend pitiable lives in abusive, unhappy marriages. We come across disturbing stories, often, where a woman chose to end her life rather than end an unhappy marriage. What a travesty!

As a society, we must strive to change this. True liberation shall be achieved only when women can steer their lives freely and not be bogged down by social expectations of looking a certain way, or getting married at a certain age or becoming a mother, until they choose it for themselves. Women can achieve their true potential only when these rigid norms stop placing artificial limits on their identity. They should grow up with more and more women leaders, so they don't get conditioned to think of a man as a leader. The new generation of women should grow up seeing caregiving, cleaning, cooking being an equal responsibility of both men and women. Till we can achieve that, our quest for an equal world won't end. I believe that before we can achieve an equal workplace, it is imperative to achieve equality at home, and equality in society with no limiting stigma. Before breaking the glass ceiling, we must overcome these glass fences.

While in the last century human race made great advancements and created technological marvels, women, half of this race, were and are still fighting it out for equal treatment, equal acknowledgment of their being. It makes one wonder, had half our race not been battling for the bare equality, we might have advanced tremendously more. As a generation that is reaping the fruits of the battles fought by previous generation of fighters, it is our moral duty to not relent in this fight for equality. We walk, because they stood up. Now we've to ensure that the coming generations can run on equal-footing with men, with no added hurdles along the way. They call us the "fairer" sex; let us have a society that's fair. To us.

Yet I thrive - Poetry

- Maitridevi Sisodia

Mocked and silenced,

Yet I strive,

Bruised and battered,

Yet I thrive.

It's a man's world

Yet I strive,

Odds rigged against me,

Yet I thrive

Glass fences at every life stage,

Yet I strive,

Glass ceilings to be shattered every day,

Yet I thrive.

Armed with compassion and courage,

I rise, I strive and I thrive.

Fiery sea - Poetry

- Maitridevi Sisodia

I might burn with the rage of a hundred suns,

But you'd see the calm of a thousand moons,

You couldn't drown
my voice under a hundred trumpets,

For even my soft sigh is heard over them,

You try to cage me under a thousand shackles,

But I sail like a silken cloud in the sky.

Unbent in the face of the unending battles,

Unbowed in the face of the several storms,

A fiery sea contained in a drop a serenity,

Dare you to call me the weaker sex, again.

www.ingramcontent.com/pod-product-compliance
Lightning Source LLC
LaVergne TN
LVHW051531170726
843492LV00006B/1713